Praise for Tawny Weber

"Sexy, hot, intriguing as well as fun are all
hallmarks of a Tawny Weber tale."
—*CataRomance*

"If you like laugh out loud tales laced with
spicy scenes, I recommend Tawny Weber.
I look forward to reading more from
this talented author."
—*Romance Junkies*

"Tawny Weber delivers a story that is sexy,
romantic, and inspirational. I will be
very much looking forward to more
from this talented author."
—*Wild On Books*

"*Feels Like the First Time* is scandalous fun for
the voracious reader. The story moves quickly,
smoothly, and with enough heat to burn your
fingers as you turn the pages."
—*A Romance Review*

"Snappy, young and hip, Tawny Weber's
fresh voice pops with energy!"
—*New York Times* bestselling author
Julie Elizabeth Leto

Blaze

Dear Reader,

I'm a big fan of dreaming. I dream up stories. I dream up excuses. I dream up wild scenarios in which delicious chocolate is fat-free, killer heels don't hurt my feet and money really does grow on trees.

In other words, I spend a great deal of time in a fantasy land. Which is why I was so excited when my editor suggested I write a Forbidden Fantasy. What's better than a fantasy, after all? Especially a fantasy that's naughty and off-limits....

And that's exactly what Drucilla decides her vacation-fling fantasy will be—very, very naughty. Especially when she meets surfer boy Alex, a guy who's so much more than he seems.

If you're on the Internet, please drop by my Web site at www.tawnyweber.com and let me know what you think of Drucilla and Alex's story. While you're there, check out my blog, vote for the hunk of the month or enter my current contest. I'd love to hear from you.

Enjoy,

Tawny Weber

Tawny Weber

RIDING THE WAVES

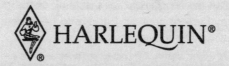

HARLEQUIN®

TORONTO • NEW YORK • LONDON
AMSTERDAM • PARIS • SYDNEY • HAMBURG
STOCKHOLM • ATHENS • TOKYO • MILAN • MADRID
PRAGUE • WARSAW • BUDAPEST • AUCKLAND

Recycling programs
for this product may
not exist in your area.

ISBN-13: 978-0-373-79568-0

RIDING THE WAVES

This edition published by arrangement with Harlequin Books S.A.

For questions and comments about the quality of this book please contact us at Customer_eCare@Harlequin.ca.

® and TM are trademarks of the publisher. Trademarks indicated with ® are registered in the United States Patent and Trademark Office, the Canadian Trade Marks Office and in other countries.

www.eHarlequin.com

Printed in U.S.A.

ABOUT THE AUTHOR

Tawny Weber is usually found dreaming up stories in her California home, surrounded by dogs, cats and kids. When she's not writing hot, spicy stories for Harlequin Blaze, she's shopping for the perfect pair of shoes or drooling over Johnny Depp pictures (when her husband isn't looking, of course). Come by and visit her on the web at www.tawnyweber.com.

Books by Tawny Weber

HARLEQUIN BLAZE
324—DOUBLE DARE
372—DOES SHE DARE?
418—RISQUÉ BUSINESS
462—COMING ON STRONG
468—GOING DOWN HARD
492—FEELS LIKE THE FIRST TIME
513—BLAZING BEDTIME STORIES, VOLUME III
       "You Have to Kiss a Lot of Frogs..."

A huge hug and lots of thanks to
Nancy Haddock for the surf instructions and to
Lisa Spindler for being my science go-to gal.

And, as always, thanks to Elaine English
for the great direction and advice.

1

"Sooo? How was your date?"

Drucilla Robichoux froze, her spoonful of lemon yogurt halfway to her mouth. She'd been dreading this question.

Wrinkling her nose, she shot a quick glance around the lab's lunchroom. Sunlight, filtered through typical San Francisco fog, dully lit the empty space. Seeing no escape—and fortunately nobody to overhear—she sighed, licked the tart yogurt from the spoon and prepared to confess.

"I think I'd be better off giving up on men," she admitted to her best friend and fellow scientist, Nikki Hanson. "This is the sixth failed dating experiment this year. And it's only August."

"I can't say I'm surprised. I still can't believe you went on more than one date with Dr. Uptight," Nikki said as she polished off her pastrami sandwich. She meant Bryan Smith-Updike, a physicist from the Lawrence Livermore Lab and Drucilla's companion the last four Saturday nights. The first three, they'd attended the theater, the opera and the California Academy of Sciences. She'd been bored to death, but not nearly as bored as she'd been during the sex that'd marked their fourth weekend.

"It wasn't much of a date," Dru admitted. "The guy was a gasper."

"That's even worse than the wheezer. What was his name? Mad-scientist Maxwell?"

"No, he was the counter. You know, in-two-three. Out-two-three. The wheezer was that biochemist I dated last year."

"Maybe gasping is a step up?" Nikki asked, her doubtful wince making her dimples flash. "But at least Uptight finally dropped drawers, right?"

"Unfortunately," Drucilla confirmed with a grimace. She puffed out her cheeks, contemplated the last few bites of yogurt, then shoved it aside and opened her bag of cut vegetables.

She lamented the sad truth…. Her love life was in an unending downward spiral of suckiness.

Drucilla wanted to love sex. Better yet, she wanted a sex life worth loving. She was a firm believer in maintaining a healthy balance between mind and body. Her mind was top-notch and she worked to keep her body the same. Good food, regular exercise. And sex, dammit. She'd read plenty of studies that claimed that regular, satisfying sex was important to good health. And she was missing out.

Maybe self-gratification would be enough if she increased her beta-carotene intake?

"So the date didn't go well?" Nikki nudged, obviously wanting all the dirty details.

Drucilla popped a cherry tomato in her mouth and debated blowing off the question. Then, realizing it couldn't sound any worse than the wheezer confession—always nice to have a rock bottom—she shrugged.

"Oh, sure, it went well for him," she said after she'd swallowed. "Peachy, in fact. Remember how I told you that Bryan's been frustrated with the calculations he's been working on?" Drucilla waited for Nikki's confused nod before continuing.

"Well, he's had a breakthrough. Mid, shall we say, thrust, he yelled 'Eureka!' rolled over and scrambled for his pants, where he apparently always carries a notepad and pen."

Dru smirked at the shocked, slack-jawed look on Nikki's face. "Yep, he was so thrilled to have broken that mathematical code, he didn't even grumble when I shoved him out the door before he could finish zipping his pants."

Mouth still agape, Nikki shook her head in pitying shock. "How on earth do you find these guys?"

"It's a gift," Dru mused.

"I think this guy's worse than that Nobel laureate you went out with who carried a picture of Einstein in his pocket along with a condom."

"And insisted on both during sex," Dru agreed, wrinkling her nose at the memory. "The condom was welcome, but sadly, the only one of the three of us to end up with wild-sex hair was ole Al."

And only to Nikki would Dru confess such a thing. Years of moving from town to town—her parents usually on the run from creditors—on top of Dru's own innate shyness, had made it difficult for her to make friends. Even college, or colleges since she'd attended four, had been spent on the move, with Dru having to hold down three jobs to pay for school and living at home to cut expenses.

But when she'd come to work at Trifecta, Nikki had taken Dru under her wing. Now Nikki was her best friend and one of the few people she worked with whom she also saw socially. The lab, National Physics Trifecta, was a brain trust that specialized in the three branches of physics: astro, nuclear and quantum. While Dru was all about the astro, Nikki—despite her sweet dimples and luxurious black curls—was nicknamed the ball breaker of the quantum physics lab.

Not only was she in a different department from Dru, Nikki was almost a different species. Optimistic, upbeat and outgoing, with a curvy figure that turned men's heads, the brunette was Dru's polar opposite.

Blond, cool and contained, Dru knew she put off a don't-touch-me air. She didn't mean to, but couldn't seem to change it. So she'd had to find a way to make it work for her. She'd finally figured that if she held her head high and remembered to make at least one friendly comment a day, she was fine. Now everyone at the lab thought she was just reserved, offering respect and a level of deference she knew was rare, given her age and nonleadership position.

And to keep that respect, it was vital that any and all details of her miserable love life remain private.

It helped that the lab had very stringent interpersonal-relationship rules. Friendships were fine, but dating was frowned on. Not that Dru would ever date anyone she actually had to work with. She'd seen too many relationships crash and burn. And somehow, while the guy managed to waltz away with his career intact, the woman always paid a price.

Because nothing, not even her bashfulness or a lack of partner-generated orgasms, would get in the way of her career security. She couldn't afford to let it. And so far, that strategy was working quite well.

Now to figure out how to make her love life work, too.

After years of bad dates, she'd finally decided to approach dating as a hypothesis. She carefully chose men who were her intellectual equal based on the premise that all men had the same basic equipment and drive. Given that the brain was the largest erogenous zone, she was sure intellectual stimulation was just as vital as clitoral stimulation in achieving sexual satisfaction.

At least, she'd been pretty sure. It was damn hard to test a theory if all the guys she dated had the sexual skills of a ninth-grade nerd with a *National Geographic* fetish.

It was enough to make a woman question her hypothesis. To say nothing of her ability to ever have a decent sex life.

"Okay, so the sex has been a little, well, lousy. But don't give up on men," Nikki said, breaking through Dru's dismal realizations with forced cheer. "What about Kyle, that new guy in the lab? He's cute, in a horn-rimmed sort of way."

Dru was shaking her head before Nikki even finished the sentence.

"He's also a coworker. You know how Dr. Shelby feels about fraternization. If I started dating, or worse, having lousy sex, with the guys here, word would get around. It'd haunt me. My private life would be fodder for the water cooler chitchat. And any success I have, people would wonder who I slept with to get there."

Nikki gave her a long look, trying to poke a hole in that excuse. Finally she shrugged and said, "We don't have water coolers."

Dru rolled her eyes.

"Look, why don't you quit the geeks and go for a hottie?" Nikki suggested, wiping her mouth before opening a bag of corn chips. Dru's mouth watered. Whether it was over the chips or the visual of hottie-sex, she didn't know.

Ignoring the drool collecting in the corners of her lips, she reminded herself of the five pounds she'd been trying to lose since New Year's and said, "Because boredom makes for poor foreplay?"

Which she knew firsthand, since the last three guys she'd dated had almost foreplayed her to sleep. And God knew she'd be the ultimate snoozefest to some poor guy who didn't talk science. It went back to that shyness thing. If she was talking shop, she was fine. Social chitchat? Zzzz.

"Oh, my God, Dru. What does a guy have to do? Discuss the theory of relativity while going down on you? You need to disconnect your brain from your—"

"Okay," Dru interrupted before Nikki could start naming parts of her anatomy. "I get your point. But I don't agree. I really believe that unless we have common interests, there's no point in dating or having sex—albeit lousy sex—with a guy."

"There are other things to talk about than science, you know," Nikki snapped, the frustration creasing her brow echoed in her tone.

Dru wasn't about to open the door to another conversation about her social skills. The last time she'd cracked it open by mentioning that she didn't know how to dance, Nikki had forced her to spend twelve Saturdays at dance clubs. Talk about misery squared.

"Look, even if I wanted to research alternate dating pools, when do I have time?" she protested, her tone making it clear she'd rather be staked naked to the astronomy tower during a public meteor-shower tour.

"You know I'm already working fifty hours a week. I help my mom on weekends. The cosmic string project starts next month and as soon as—" not *if*, she refused to consider failure "—I get the grant, I'll be so busy I won't have time to masturbate, let alone date."

"A woman always has time to masturbate," Nikki intoned.

Dru shrugged, waving her carrot stick in surrender before snapping off a bite.

"Sooo…" Nikki drew the word out as she carefully wiped her fingers on a napkin.

"So… What?" Dru asked, not liking the glint in her friend's chocolate-brown eyes.

"So, I have an idea."

Just as she would if a student was about to pitch a half-baked astrological theory, Dru folded her hands on the table, arched her brow and gave Nikki a patient, you-are-probably-insane look.

"Take a vacation."

The knots in Dru's shoulders unwound. Well, that wasn't too crazy.

"Someplace totally away from here, completely relaxing and extremely decadent."

A vision of sand, surf and sun filled her imagination. Wouldn't that be glorious?

"Mmm, maybe I'll book a cruise or something this summer," Dru murmured. An entire week filled with strappy sandals, rich food and sarong-covered bikinis while she read by the water. Heaven. "I've always wanted to visit Cancún. Or maybe the Bahamas."

"No. Now. Next week, before your schedule turns crazy with the grant interviews and the guest lecturer and this upcoming project that will bury you in seventy-hour weeks."

Unspoken was Nikki's belief that Dru would make excuses and not take a vacation. But the message was clear in the stubborn set of her jaw.

Before Dru could talk her off the lunatic-ledge, Glenn Shelby, Trifecta's director, bounced into the lunchroom. The older man was the epitome of enthusiasm, always. His nothing-is-impossible attitude was supposed to be an inspiration to his teams. Most of them wanted to spike his morning fruit smoothie with sleeping pills.

Dru's gaze jumped from his face to the stubborn glee on Nikki's, then back to their boss, who was offering his usual chipper lunch greeting.

"No," she mouthed at Nikki, tension wrapping tight over her shoulders. The road to success was not lined with spur-of-the-moment vacation requests or inconveniences to the boss.

Nikki, of course, ignored her.

"Glenn, Dru needs a vacation."

"Vacation? Now?"

Well, that had certainly punctured his enthusiastic recitation of the joys of fresh-squeezed orange juice. His words all came out in a gulp.

It was all she could do not to drop her face into her hands. With an almost silent hiss of protest, Dru glared at Nikki.

"Don't worry about it, Dr. Shelby. I know we're too busy right now. Nikki knows it, too."

Nikki didn't even have the grace to give Dru an apologetic look before shoving her off the cliff.

"Glenn, you know Dru is leading the cosmic string project that kicks off next month. It's vital that we make a good showing for Trifecta, isn't it?" Nikki didn't wait for his answer, or act as if she saw the glare Dru was trying to melt her with, she just plowed ahead. "But here's the thing. I don't think she's had a vacation in, oh, forever. Weren't you just saying last week that a rested mind is an alert mind?"

The director shot Dru a measuring look through the bifocals he'd perched on his egg-shaped head. From the frown that washed over his face, his X-ray vision found her health deteriorating at a rapid pace.

"Yes, yes, good point. We want everyone in top form next month. All the departments have major projects launching, but yours is the most vital, Robichoux. After all, it's not every year we get such a distinguished guest as A. A. Maddow as a project leader."

Assistant leader, Dru wanted to protest. For the first time, she was project leader. But the road to success wasn't lined with divas, either, so she sucked it up and shot Nikki an icy glare instead. Nikki grinned.

"I highly recommend Los Cabos if you're looking for a beach setting," Dr. Shelby said, taking his Healthy Choice lunch from the microwave and heading for the door. "A.A.

himself suggested it to me when we agreed to his contract. He was right, as usual. Los Cabos was both relaxing and rejuvenating. You'll enjoy it."

Then he was gone, the door swinging closed with a loud *swoosh*.

And that was that. Dru briefly considered chasing him down and voicing her objections over his low-cal chicken à l'orange, but she knew it was pointless. After all, A. A. Maddow was the rock star of the science world. A Wolf Award nominee and brilliant physicist, he was going to be working alongside Drucilla for the next three months. His input was apparently vital, in Glenn's mind, to both clarify her theory and convince the grant committee that a small lab like Trifecta was worthy of huge sums of money.

The director wouldn't want to risk anyone on his staff being less than sparkling for the grand appearance.

"I can't believe you did that," Dru said, gathering her lunch wrappers in tight, efficient moves.

"You can thank me with a nice souvenir," Nikki told her as she sauntered back to the table, her teeth flashing white as she grinned.

"Thank you? I want to beat you with your own corn-chip bag," Dru snapped before she could control herself. She sucked in a deep breath, then said in her most reasonable tone, "I have responsibilities and commitments, Nikki. I don't have time to sip margaritas and hit the beach."

"That's not all I want you to hit," Nikki said with a stern frown. Dru figured that must be the look the woman used to keep her hunky new husband in line.

But Drucilla Antoinette was made of stronger stuff than that. So she just leaned back in her chair and raised a brow.

"You need a man."

"Isn't that where this conversation started?"

"My point exactly. You need a hot man. A hunky, yummy, no-discussion-needed, orgasm-at-first-sight man."

Dru's breath caught somewhere between her chest and her throat at that image.

"No, I'm only looking to relax," she protested. Not willing to consider something as clichéd as a vacation fling, she got up to cross the room and toss her garbage away. As if she wanted to get rid of the tempting image Nikki had put in her head.

"What's more relaxing than an uninhibited sexual escapade?" her friend asked behind her.

And where better to have a sexual escapade than far away from her day-to-day world, on vacation from work and distanced from the rules she surrounded her life with?

Dru stepped over to the sink to wash her hands. The water rushed over her, cooling flesh that suddenly felt as if it was on fire. She watched the clear liquid flow, her mind filled with images of hot beach sex with a well-muscled beach bum.

"I can't deliberately set out to have a fling," she murmured.

"Why on earth not? You need to let go of this thing you have for only doing brainiacs, Dru. No intelligence litmus test. Just pure, sexual attraction. You find a guy who turns you on and have a week's worth of wild monkey sex."

"To what purpose?" Dru asked as she dried her hands, considering the ramifications of giving in to the ultimate temptation. If she did it away from the lab, nobody would see her choice. Nobody would judge her for picking a hot guy whose only purpose was to satisfy her every lusting need. She wouldn't be deemed a sex-crazed idiot who made bad choices in the name of screaming orgasms. Her breath shuddered. God, what did a screaming orgasm actually feel like?

Dru saw the smirk on Nikki's face and clarified, "What's the purpose, besides sex?"

"Does there have to be another purpose? For once, go after a guy who turns you on. Not one you have to convince yourself is sexy." Nikki gave her a wicked grin, her dimples flashing as she came over to rinse her lunch dishes. "Find a guy with the stamina to go all night. A hunky horndog who'll worship your body."

The image flashed, erotic and intense. A faceless young stud, his muscles oiled and gleaming in the moonlight, poised over her body as he acted out her every kinky fantasy. She swallowed and shifted, glad her lab coat covered her aching nipples. Panicked, Dru scanned the room, even though she knew nobody else was there to overhear.

This was a crazy idea. Completely insane.

So what did that say about her for even considering it?

As if she sensed Dru was weakening, Nikki laid her hand on Dru's arm and offered a wicked smile. "Girlfriend, it's time to find yourself a playmate."

Two WEEKS LATER Dru paid the taxi driver and waited while the bellboy loaded her suitcases onto a cart. She used the time to look around.

Los Cabos, Mexico. Oceanfront luxury with the charm of old-world Mexico. White sandy beaches, the Sea of Cortez, ocean breezes and beautiful tropical foliage.

Tension she hadn't even realized she'd hoarded in her shoulders drained away. Far from the San Francisco breeze, Dru felt freer than she'd ever been. Here, nobody knew her. She didn't have to worry about projecting the right image, about climbing the ladder or about the anchoring weight of family responsibilities that kept her pushing for success.

She was here to take a break.

Dr. Shelby had raved about both the relaxing atmosphere and the beautiful views.

And he'd been right.

When she found herself checking out the bellboy's ass, Dru rolled her eyes. That probably wasn't the kind of view her boss had meant.

Forcing her gaze to stay on the guy's shoulders, broad and muscular as they were, she followed him and her luggage into the hotel to the reservations desk.

Thirty minutes later, she'd changed out of her practical travel clothes—a button-down shirt and khaki pants—and into an eye-wateringly bright floral sundress and had defiantly unbraided her long hair. The practical voice in her head argued that it'd just get tangled on the beach. She didn't care. She figured freedom came with a few tangles.

Dru stepped out the back door of her bungalow and gasped. There, spread before her, was the most gorgeous beach she'd ever seen. Sand, soft and inviting, swept from as far as the eye could see. Beyond it the ocean, dark blue in the early-evening light, beat frothy white waves against the dull gold of the shore.

Just the sight of it filled her with a mellow sort of empowerment. Maybe it was the watercolor richness of the sky, purples bleeding into orange-tinged pink as the sun set behind the water. Or the wild intensity of the waves, their salty scent and roaring sound inviting her to come closer.

Or maybe it was just knowing she could do whatever she wanted. And what she wanted was to feel that water on her toes. Not bothering to go inside for her sandals, Dru skipped lightly down the wooden steps leading from her tiny patio to the still-warm sand.

Reveling in the feel of the tiny grains shifting around her feet, she headed straight for the water. It wasn't until she was halfway there that she saw him.

Her heart, and her feet, stopped.

Her mouth went as dry as the sand clinging to her ankles. She didn't blink when the soft breeze sent tendrils of her hair into her eyes, just batted it away so it didn't interfere with her view.

Oh. My. God.

He was incredible. Like some water god, he flew over the waves. The water glistened on his golden skin like diamonds in the fading light. Arms outstretched, biceps glinting as he balanced on the deep purple surfboard. Was he real? A figment of her lusty imagination? The manifestation of her every sexual fantasy? Dru's breath came in long, labored bursts. She was afraid to blink, fearing he'd disappear.

Her fingers itched to touch that bare chest, to run down the dusting of dark hair that perfectly highlighted his well-muscled abs. She stared as he got closer to shore, watching him shift his knees to a low crouch as he rode the wave all the way to the beach.

There was something so amazing about surfers. She'd always imagined them to be fearless. Able to embrace anything life handed them and ride it to success.

And talk about muscle control. That was the kind of guy who could rock against-a-wall sex and not drop the woman as she melted in orgasmic glory all over him.

Was he real? Or had her sex-deprived imagination conjured up the perfect man to fulfill her lusty desires?

About thirty feet away, she watched him walk across the sand. This close, she could see how young he was. Mid-twenties at the most. His dripping hair fell in inky black curls around his head, his beautiful face adding to the image of a Greek god come to life.

He stopped at the brightly decorated surf-shop bungalow, and she watched him key in a code, then open the door and store his board. His familiarity made it obvious he wasn't a guest. Did he work at the surf shop? Or at the hotel?

Whatever he did, he was obviously out of her league. Not that it mattered. It wasn't as if a sweet young thing like him would have any interest in an almost thirty-year-old scientist with social anxieties and repressed sexual needs.

Needs she'd been perfectly fine ignoring until Nikki had gotten her all riled up over her ridiculous ideas. Dru had no idea how to flirt, how to attract a man's attention. Especially not a man like that. No matter what Nikki had suggested, Dru wasn't here for a fling.

Except here he was. The most incredible man she'd ever seen. A man who would definitely not stop midthrust, but know how to bring a woman to a screaming orgasm, then make her writhe and beg for more.

And then he turned. Their eyes met. Dru's breath lodged somewhere between her aching nipples and her dry mouth. His gaze holding her captive from twenty feet away, one corner of his mouth quirked in a charmingly adorable little-boy grin.

And he walked toward her. Frozen in the sand, Drucilla didn't know if she should pull back her shoulders, stick out her chest and smile beguilingly. Or turn on her bare heel and run like hell.

2

ALEX MADDOW GAVE a quick shake of his head, his hair flying around his face as the drops of water scattered. The exhilaration of riding the waves still surged through his body. He filled his lungs with the salty evening air and gave a deep sigh of satisfaction.

There was nothing like surfing at sunset. The colors of the sky, the feel of the cooling air as it whipped around his body while he flew over the water. *Incredible* was the only word for it. God, he felt great.

Then he saw her. There, a glowing jewel against the pristine white adobe of the hotel. Talk about incredible. Simply stunning. Despite the aftereffects of the cold water, he stirred in hardening awareness. Images flooded his mind of naked bodies, breathy moans and exquisite pleasure.

He was never a man to deny his sexual needs, but Alex usually knew the woman's name before he planned the many different ways he'd enjoy her body. Then again, he'd never experienced this intense, instantaneous lust-at-first-sight reaction to a woman before, either.

His eyes narrowed. She reminded him of one of those elfish princesses his mother used to read him stories about—the ones he'd always fallen in love with. Tall and slender, and her angular face commanded attention. Silvery-blond hair waved around her shoulders in a silken cape. The demureness of the cut of her calf-length sundress was at odds with the vivid turquoise-and-pink pattern. Bare toes curled sensually in the sand.

A slow smile of anticipation curved Alex's lips. It was as if it was meant to be. From one exhilarating ride to the temptation of another. Never let it be said that Albert Alexander Maddow didn't appreciate opportunity when fate placed it right in front of him. Especially an opportunity that stole his breath away, filling his mind with sexual challenge.

Through wasting time, he strode across the sand toward her, shoving his wet curls off his face as he moved. The closer he got, the more intrigued he was. Not because of her looks, but because of the look she was giving him. As though she couldn't decide if he was a crazed ax murderer or how he'd taste covered in chocolate.

From the set of her chin and the way she shifted her body, lifting one shoulder and crossing her arms over her chest, she obviously figured she could handle either option. Alex grinned. There was nothing sexier than a confident woman.

And she was even better up close. Her brows, shades darker than her hair, slashed a strong arch over eyes so blue they were almost the same purple as the sunset. Her mouth was narrow, the upper lip heavier than the lower. He wanted to nibble on that lip, to run his tongue over it and see if it was as delicious as it looked.

Had he ever been so intensely, instantly attracted to a woman? Alex couldn't recall and didn't care. After all, the only thing that mattered was this moment and this woman.

Until the moment was over.

"Gorgeous," he commented when he was a couple feet away from her. Her features didn't add up to pretty individually, but put together, they were stunning. His fingers ached to trace the line of her throat down to the gentle swell of flesh pressing against the vivid floral cotton of her dress.

"The surf?" she asked after a brief hesitation. Even her voice was sexy. Low and husky, at odds with her ethereal appearance.

"The view," he clarified, sensing that she wouldn't appreciate surfeit flirtation. A man who prided himself on his intuition as much as his brains, he reined in his instinct to hit hard.

She obviously wasn't fooled, though. She arched one brow, then glanced over his shoulder. He followed her gaze, taking in the watercolor beauty of the sunset. As always, the sight centered him. The ever-changing transformations of the sea never failed to fill his soul with peace.

She got that, he realized as his gaze traced the lines of her face. She didn't look like a woman used to peace, but one who did appreciate it when it was there in front of her.

"It must feel amazing to be a part of that," she said with a nod of her chin toward the pounding sea. She acted as if she wasn't aware of his attraction, but the stiffness of her shoulders and slight step she took backward told him otherwise.

She didn't leave, though. Which said it all, in his mind.

"Do you surf?" he asked, already knowing the answer. She had that romantic, wouldn't-it-be-an-adventure look in her eyes. Not that surfing wasn't both romantic and adventurous. But when a surfer looked at the sea, there was always an underlying layer of respect.

"I never have surfed before, no," she said, her gaze meeting his again. There was a summing-up, a calculation in her eyes. He recognized the look. Felt the sexual pull of it tugging at him. It was the kind of expression that said she wondered how he'd look without his swim trunks and could he keep it up long enough to make her scream with pleasure.

Then, as if realizing he'd caught the look, she blinked. Color, soft pale pink, swept over her cheeks. But she didn't drop her gaze. Almost defiantly, she kept those indigo eyes on his.

A slow, challenging grin spread over his face. He would enjoy showing her both the view and his talents.

"Surfing is like sex," he told her softly. "An intense ride on a lover that knows how to push you to your limits, then bring you back to earth with a gentle kiss and an invitation to ride again."

He waited to see if she'd blush a second time.

"You don't say." Her sharp cheekbones blush free, she gave him a long, cool look, then shook her head. "Somehow I doubt that tempting promise of pleasure is quite the same for a beginner. I'd imagine there's a lot more flailing around, falling and inhaling seawater."

"Not if you have the right teacher," he assured her, taking a small step closer. The sand shifted under his bare feet. He inhaled deeply. Her perfume filled his senses, even from a foot away. Was it stronger along her throat? If he buried his face in the curve, just where her breasts started to swell, would it overwhelm him?

"I might look into surf lessons while I'm here," she evaded, not taking the sex-talk bait.

"I'll teach you."

She gave a nervous little laugh, the sound saying she'd just bet he would. A shutter dropped, her expression chilling almost as much as his body as the evening breeze teased the water still coating his skin.

"It's okay," he assured her, figuring she was smart to ice up. He was a stranger, after all. For now. "The Surf Shack is a part of the hotel's offering. I teach for them."

She didn't appear to be reassured. Not sure why, Alex put on his safest, most trustworthy face. The kind he hoped seemed nonthreatening. Even though he wanted to go in the opposite direction, he took a tiny step back. He instantly missed the scent of her perfume, flowery and rich, over the salty scent of the ocean.

"You can check at the hotel. Just ask anyone about Alex and surfing. They'll vouch for me." He was pretty sure the last time he'd come this close to begging a woman to spend time with him occurred when he was sixteen and trying to find a date to his first college formal.

Still, she hesitated. Her gaze slid from his face to the Surf Shack, a tiny frown furrowing the alabaster skin between those deep blue eyes.

He saw the refusal on her lips.

"Just say maybe," he suggested before she could say anything.

Humor flashed in those stunning eyes and she raised one brow, then shrugged.

"Maybe," she murmured. Then, without another word, not even a yes-I-want-to-do-you-until-we-both-get-sand-burns look, she turned away.

He watched her go, rubbing a hand over the bruised ache in his chest and wondering what the hell had just happened. He felt as if he'd been smacked upside the head with his board in a total wipeout disaster—exhilarated, confused and wondering if he'd done permanent damage.

Crazy, he told himself. Women were many things. Alluring, captivating, desirable. They were fun, felt incredible and made perfect temporary companions.

But dangerous?

He shook his head, his damp curls falling over his eyes a reminder that he'd better get them cut before he reported in for his real job at the end of the month.

Dangerous, he thought again. Nah.

There was nothing risky about making time with a

stunning blonde who had a yen to learn the magic of the ocean. The only thing at stake was a little time and the possibility of some righteously awesome sex.

SITTING AT THE HOTEL'S dining patio basking in the sunshine the next morning, Dru sipped her coffee. The rich aroma filled her senses. Dark, robust and strong. The perfect accompaniment to her decadent breakfast—stuffed French toast, chorizo and spicy fried potatoes.

All favorites, all bad for her. Exactly what she needed to start this vacation right, she thought with a sigh as she set her coffee cup down. Especially after waking from the most incredibly hot, orgasmic dream she'd ever experienced.

Vivid images of her and the gorgeous man from the beach doing it in wicked abandon on his surfboard filled her mind. She shifted in her wicker chair and wished the waiter would come over and refill her ice water. She definitely needed to cool off.

She hadn't been able to get the sexy surf god out of her mind, and obviously her subconscious had put his image and all Nikki's talk about vacation flings together and served her up a montage of sensual impressions. Since the dream-induced orgasm had rocked, she wasn't going to knock it.

A chorus of greetings, in both English and Spanish, rang out along the edge of the dining patio. Dru pulled her attention away from the ocean to glance at the commotion.

As if her musings had conjured him, the sexy surf god of her dreams sauntered up the tile steps and greeted both guests and hotel staff.

Dru's breath tripped, her pulse racing. He was even better in sunlight. She'd spent half the night telling herself it was the romance of the surf and moonlight that had made him look like a Greek god. That, and the mostly naked expanse of delicious male flesh she'd been mesmerized by.

But no, even with that gorgeous chest covered by a pristine white T-shirt, he was still the tastiest-looking thing she'd seen all morning. She took a sip of her water, needing to wet her lips and afraid to add any more caffeine to her already racing heart rate.

He seemed familiar with everyone. Obviously he'd been telling the truth when he'd said he worked for the hotel. She shifted in her chair, trying to ease the building pressure between her suddenly damp thighs.

As if she were sitting at the table, Nikki's voice chimed in Drucilla's head: *Go for it. He's hot, he's sexy. He's perfect vacation-fling material.*

Just like the night before, she didn't know if she should listen to the voice—and her body's urgings—or run like hell.

Then his eyes met hers. He murmured something to the people circling him. Then, a wide, wicked grin on his face, he crossed the patio. A tilt of his chin toward the waiter had him a cup of coffee before he reached her table.

"May I join you?" he asked,

Nerves, from both sexual awareness and her ever-present shyness, flooded her system. Despite the little voice urging her to run, she waved her hand toward the empty seat across from her in invitation.

"I didn't introduce myself last night. I'm Alex," he said, sliding into the chair and helping himself to one of the blueberry muffins in the basket on her table.

"Drucilla," she said, automatically offering her hand to shake.

Mistake, she realized as he took her fingers in his. Warmth, with its hypnotically sexy pull, poured from his palm into hers. Her body tried to melt, right there into his hand. A puddle of lust over the breakfast table.

No, not going there, she scolded herself as she tugged her

hand away. Needing to cool off at the thought, she reached
for her ice water.

"Did you sleep well, Drucilla?"

Had he peeked into her mind to know she'd tossed and
turned in sweaty homage to the dream orgasm he'd given
her? She almost choked on her water. Calling herself silly,
Dru brushed the thought aside and gave him a little shrug
and a smile.

"I rarely sleep easily my first night after traveling," she
excused.

"You should have let me help," he told her, popping the
second half of the muffin into his mouth.

"Somehow I think your help would have done more to keep
me up than make me sleep," she said with a nervous laugh.
He was actually flirting with her. Excitement spun through
her system, its rapid trajectory hindered by the terror flying
along with it.

"Oh, no, intense physical exertion is excellent for bringing
on deep sleep. Didn't you know that?"

His grin was a dare. She knew it. Even though she didn't
have a chance in hell of handling the dare, she still couldn't
resist.

"I'd heard the rumor. But from what I understand," she
said, leaning forward, both hands clenched—in both nerves
and excitement—in her lap, "the exertion has to actually be
good. Mediocre is just a lesson in frustration, isn't it?"

"Mediocre isn't even worth doing," he agreed. His eyes
had dropped, just for a second, to her breasts. Hotter than
the overhead sun, they warmed her. Filled her with sexual
power like she'd never experienced. It felt…incredible.

"My point exactly," she said.

"Well, there you go," he returned with a wicked grin. "You
should have let me help."

"And how do I know you're good?" she challenged, unsure

where the nerve to flirt was coming from. But since she seemed to be doing it right, she wasn't about to question the gift.

"References, of course."

Dru couldn't help it, she burst out laughing. She knew he wanted her to think he was talking about sex. And she figured on one level, they were. What would he do if she called his bluff? Not sure she was ready to find out, she played it safe instead.

"Of course," she said as if his response was perfectly reasonable.

"You can always take me up on it tonight," he offered. The look on his face was pure sexual challenge. Dru knew damn well he could rise to the challenge, too. In every sense. This was a guy who didn't need the likes of Albert Einstein to get his groove on.

"I'm not sure yet that I'm interested in learning to surf," she told him, ending the double-entendre exchange with an apologetic little shrug.

His quick frown said he hadn't been ready for it to end, though.

"Is this a game?" he asked, his expression pleasant. But she still heard the hint of irritation in his tone.

"I don't play games."

Alex laughed, his amusement lightly tinged with disbelief.

She leaned back in her chair, resting one elbow on the arm, and arched an inquiring brow. The look she gave him demanded an explanation.

After all, he was the one who'd plopped himself down at her table and helped himself to her muffin.

His laughter trailed off. He gave her a long stare, his dark eyes narrowed in contemplation. "I'm sorry. I guess I'm a little confused. I'm not used to such unclear signals from a woman. I'm obviously interested in you. I'd like to spend some time together, get to know you better. Much, much better."

Dru's heart pounded, a tingling kind of fear moving through her body. So much for beating around the bush. Alex was the most direct, in-her-face man she'd ever met.

It only made him sexier.

"I thought that's what we were doing." Although clearly not as much as he, or she, for that matter, would like.

"You know what I mean," he said, brushing aside her socially correct reply.

Dru bit her lip. Wasn't this proof perfect that she shouldn't try to socialize outside her milieu? Give her a brainiac, a science buff, even an amateur astronomer, she'd be fine. But a hunky guy with eyes like melted chocolate and a body worthy of a god? Throw in enough sexual tension to send a nun running for a cold shower, a misguided attempt at flirtation and what did you get? Her, feeling like a turned-on, embarrassed idiot with her pretty, floral wedge sandal stuck right there in her big mouth.

Not sure what to do about the irritation suddenly overshadowing the desire he'd sparked in her body, Drucilla tapped her fingers on the table.

"So, what?" she finally asked, figuring she'd blown it anyway so she might as well just be herself. "If a woman doesn't drop at your feet the instant she meets you, she's playing a game?"

An appreciative look flashed in his dark eyes, but he kept his face straight.

"Maybe not at my feet," he teased. "But usually there's a definite decision about whether she wants to pursue the possibility of getting better acquainted. As a rule, people know instantly if they're interested or not. Whether they'll choose to act on that interest is another thing, of course. And that's where the game usually comes in."

Dru frowned. Not over his reference to his easy conquests. That was no surprise. But at his words. They were pretty deep for a surf instructor. Then she mentally smacked herself for making such a snobbish judgment call.

"I assure you, my taking my time to decide on what I want isn't a game," she said, guilt over her thoughts making her tone more apologetic than she'd intended.

His grin, fast and sexy, told her he was more than willing to take advantage of that opening.

"What can I do to help you make up your mind?" he offered, leaning forward and putting his hand over hers as it rested on the glass table. Sparks flared. Hot, intense and almost overpowering. Energy, purely sexual, raced through her system. Her nipples beaded in instant response. If he could turn her on this easily, with just a look and a touch, what could he do to her body if she let him? And what the hell was she waiting for to find out?

Dru tried to regulate her breathing. She could tell he knew damned well the effect he had on her. The question was, what effect did she have on him? And how could she make sure it was an even exchange? Although she sucked at flirting, she wasn't totally insecure. But neither was she stupid. Alex was a gorgeous, charismatic man, he could have any woman he wanted. Since they had nothing in common, why was he hitting on her so hard?

And could she handle it if she gave in to her body's demands? If her flirtation skills were dismal, her sexual skills were even worse. The chances of humiliation were high. Was it worth it? She looked at Alex again and sighed. Oh, yeah. She was pretty sure it was.

Pretty sure. But not positive. Needing time to think it

through, she took her napkin from her lap and set it on the table.

"You're leaving?" The disappointment in his words was echoed in his expression. His eyes clearly said she'd let him down. Whether it was because he'd miss her or because she wasn't playing those games he'd referred to, she wasn't sure.

"I have some things I need to take care of," she said honestly—she considered thinking this through to be a very necessary something to take care of. "Since we've run into each other twice already in the eighteen hours I've been here, I'm sure I'll see you again."

When she did, she planned on having all her thinking finished. One way or another, she promised herself as she murmured her goodbye and swung her tote bag over her shoulder, she'd be ready for action.

ALEX WATCHED Drucilla walk away, her tidy plait of silvery hair swishing between her bare shoulder blades. Her refusal to play confused him. He'd learned his lesson young and well. Everyone, men and women, played. Hers must be a new game. One he hadn't been dealt yet. He'd figure out the rules fast enough, he was sure.

"Wipeout?"

Alex quit his contemplation of Drucilla's hips as she turned the corner back to her bungalow to glance at his friend. Juan was dressed in waiter's whites, obviously filling in to help out his parents, who owned the hotel.

"I'm still paddling," Alex quipped with a shrug. He pushed away from the table and helped Juan gather the plates and debris. "You up for hitting some waves this afternoon?"

Juan smirked at the change of subject, but he knew Alex well enough to know his friend didn't brag about women. Not while pursuing them, not while doing them, not after kissing them goodbye when it was over. Alex's momma had a saying—wherever he put his privates was meant to stay private.

And Alex always listened to his momma.

"We're short staffed," Juan said with a morose sigh as he glanced at the surfers already riding the waves.

Alex made a sympathetic sound. There was a perfect example of why he played his life so carefully. Nothing shackled a guy faster than commitments. Not that Alex blew off his responsibilities or shirked favors. He'd been raised knowing his obligations. Three generations of excellence preceded him, and he knew better than to disappoint his family.

Which was fine. He loved what he did. That was why his career was the only thing he allowed himself to commit to. And he'd arranged his life so that commitment still let him live exactly the way he wanted.

"You up for teaching some surfer wannabes this afternoon?" Juan asked as he wiped the table clean, then moved his tray to the next one. "You're covering for Manuel, right?"

"From siesta to eight," Alex confirmed. Juan's cousin Manuel ran the Surf Shack and had gone to Cozumel for the week to celebrate his *abuela*'s hundredth birthday. He had a couple kids to take care of the shack, but nobody to give lessons while he was away. Since teaching was right up Alex's alley, he'd offered to help out. On a limited basis.

"And will you be offering private lessons to the pretty blonde?" Juan teased, as always trying to break through Alex's typical reticence when it came to women.

"Maybe," Alex murmured. He caught a glimpse of electric blue and saw Drucilla making her way down the beach. A large beach bag partially concealed her vivid dress, and a huge, floppy hat covered her glorious hair.

"I chatted with her when I was taking her order," Juan continued, not noticing Alex's attention shift. "She's a smart lady. You'll be able to talk to her about anything. Unlike that surf Betty you were with last time you were here. I think her IQ was smaller than her bra size."

Juan had a bias. He called any woman who competed with him on the waves a surf Betty. Alex frowned, trying to remember his last visit, eight months ago. Then it hit him. Pretty brunette, good surfer, total beach bunny.

He grimaced. Yeah, she hadn't been the brightest. But she'd been amazing on a surfboard. On and off the waves, he remembered with an amused smile. But still, a guy liked to be able to actually converse with the woman he was with once in a while.

Few people on Los Cabos knew what Alex did in the ten months out of the year that he wasn't here surfing. Not that he was ashamed of his career. He was a damn good scientist. He'd excelled early and often, graduating college at the age most people started. A prodigy, he'd learned young to set a goal, work his ass off and make every move count. Hell, he'd earned every accolade right on down the list, all the way to his Wolf Award. As had been expected.

But that was work. And this wasn't.

"I'm on vacation," Alex excused. Besides, he never talked about his other life when he was here. He came to Los Cabos to rejuvenate. To maintain balance and stay connected to what mattered.

"She asked about you. Wanted to know what you did around here," Juan said slyly.

Alex's gaze flew to his friend's face. He took in the grin, white against dark skin, and the humor dancing in Juan's brown eyes.

"What'd you tell her?"

"That she should talk to you personally."

Alex grinned.

"She said she'd rather not."

His smile fell away. Then he snickered at his own ego. Hey, a woman like Dru, one who took a little extra effort to catch, was always worth the time and energy.

"Do me a favor," he said. "If she asks again, continue keeping it on the down low."

"So you're gonna lie to her?"

Truly shocked at the suggestion, Alex glared at his friend. "Of course not. I'm simply doing what I always do. Living in the moment. And in this moment, I'm teaching surfing and she's on vacation."

Juan smirked as he lifted his tray to his shoulder. Then he nodded toward the path Dru had taken. "You always say you're living in the moment, *amigo*. Someday you're going to meet a woman who makes you dream of tomorrow."

Alex just chuckled and slapped Juan on the shoulder as he passed by. No point in disillusioning the guy, after all. For all Alex's Zen approach to life, he was a realist. While he loved the concept of romance as much as the next guy and adored women in all their glory, he knew better than to think that forever and commitment were part of his vocabulary.

But a few days, the surf and the sunset?

He watched Drucilla spread her towel on the oversize beach chair cushion, then straighten. Her back was to him, but he could tell she'd crossed her arms over her belly. With a quick tug she pulled the electric-blue dress off, shaking her head to free her hair again. He watched the silvery-blond braid slide along her back and imagined his fingers combing through that silken length. His mouth pressing warm, soft kisses to those toned shoulders.

His gaze traced her back, bare now except for the strap of her purple bikini. Mouth dry, he took in the slender curve of her waist, the gentle swell of her hips. And those legs. His heart raced as if he was cresting a wave. What would those legs feel like wrapped around his hips? Those long

legs anchoring him tightly as he drove into the wonder of
her body?

Alex's breath whooshed out in a jagged sigh.

Yeah. A few days, the surf and the sunset. He'd be sharing all of them with Drucilla and loving every second of it.
Better yet, he'd make damn sure she loved it, too.

3

SIX HOURS LATER, Dru bit her lip, a giddy sort of terror fluttering down her back like a teasing breeze. She was crazy to be doing this. A million rational arguments competed for center stage in her mind, all telling her that she should turn heel in the sand and head right back up the dune to her bungalow.

The practical scientist in her gave a patient sigh. It wasn't as if this was going to be dangerous. It was a controlled environment with a set time limit. She was entering into the experiment with a solid, well-thought-out hypothesis.

The horny woman in her gave a disdainful eye roll. Enough with the bullshit excuses already. She was solidly in lust with Alex, and he was exactly what Nikki had suggested. A fling. The answer to all her sexual frustrations. The kind of guy who could go all night, making her gasp and writhe and scream.

She really, *really* wanted to gasp and writhe and scream.

After all, this was vacation. Wild sexual romps were practically required, right? It didn't matter that she didn't know much about him. Or that they wouldn't have anything to talk about. Nerdy her and a hunky surfer? No common ground at all. She was pretty sure she had other uses for his mouth, though. And she'd be back at work, with plenty of people to talk to soon enough.

She should just go for it, she thought as her stomach tumbled over itself and nerves made her light-headed.

"C'mon, you know you want to do it," Alex teased, the grin curving his gorgeous sun-kissed face telling her he knew she was arguing with herself over the surfing lesson. A lesson she'd been second-guessing for the last hour, ever since she'd met him at the Surf Shack to get started.

Hopefully he didn't know the details of her internal argument, though. Or that she'd be taking him up on a lot more than just the white-and-blue-striped board he was offering. Although, from his wicked grin, he very well might know exactly what she'd been thinking.

He stood there in the late-afternoon light, two surfboards stuck in the sand, one on either side of him. This section of beach was mostly deserted, the nearest people tiny images at the far end of the hotel. The sun was hot, the breeze a bare wisp of air and Alex was gorgeous.

His muscles glinted in the sunshine, the light scent of sunscreen mixing with the salt of the ocean. His simple blue trunks rode low on his hips. Her gaze trailed over the dusting of hair on his chest, gliding down his belly like an arrow pointing the way to ecstasy.

She'd have to be an idiot to walk away.

"I do want to do it," she said in a breathless rush, committing to a lot more than the lesson.

As if he realized that, the grin slid off Alex's face. His dark eyes narrowed, taking on a smoldering look of concentration. The heat of that gaze washed over her, more intense than the rays of the afternoon sun. Her breath quickened. She sucked in her bottom lip, nibbling on the soft flesh and wondering if they could toss aside the pretense of surfing and just go back to her bungalow.

"C'mon," he invited instead of following it up, though. Maybe the lurking terror in her gaze made him hesitate. "It's time. We've already waxed the boards and gone over the basics. The next step is to hit the water."

Nerves, this time having nothing to do with the sexual tension filling the air, jumped in Dru's stomach. She eyed the seven-foot-long surfboard. Then she glanced at the vivid blue water of the Sea of Cortez.

"Maybe we should go over the safety rules again," she said faintly.

Alex smiled and rubbed a reassuring hand up and down her bare arm. His touch melted her fear with an onslaught of lust. Dru's breath hitched. A look of wicked pleasure crossed Alex's face.

He trailed his hand up and down her arm again, but this time the move was slower. Softer. More tempting. Dru's heart skipped a beat, then tumbled so fast she could feel it pounding against the slick fabric of her sedate one-piece swimsuit.

His fingers traced down again, leaving a heated path in their wake. He moved closer. Just one step. That's all it took to fill her senses with him. His body's warmth. His scent. His sexual energy.

The whole world narrowed as that energy engulfed her. The sound of the surf, the heat of the sun, they faded. She stared up at his face, the olive skin and high cheekbones. His full lower lip, perfect for nibbling.

Without realizing it, her tongue slipped out to touch her upper lip. The desire in his midnight eyes intensified. But he didn't move. Dru wasn't sure if he was holding back to torture her or if he was too much of a gentleman to hit on a student.

So any moves were up to her. Her. The woman whose last successful hit on a guy had involved a lame joke about the periodic table. Dru's heart sank to join the stressed-out butterflies bouncing around in her belly.

Taking the chickenshit route, she leaned backward instead of forward. Her body screamed in fury at the denial of pleasure. As always, though, her mind was stronger. And her mind was warning her that if she didn't learn to surf, she'd fall all over Alex, do wildly unspeakable things to his body, roll off with a gasp and realize she wouldn't have a damn thing to say to him other than thank-you.

And while she had great hopes of plenty of orgasms to thank him for, the practical scientist in her insisted that they find some common ground to discuss between sexual bouts.

At least, that was her pathetic excuse.

"I guess I know the rules well enough," she murmured.

He gave her a brief, inscrutable look, then gestured to the sea.

"You'll catch on quickly once we get started." He arched his brow, making it obvious he was talking about more than just surfing. "This part of the beach gets the smaller waves, it's pretty mellow. Perfect for getting the feel of the board."

A long, rocky spit of land separated this bit of water from the vastness of the rest of the sea. Here, the water was much calmer, the waves babies compared to the huge breakers crashing off to the left of the rocks.

She wasn't reassured. She was a hardly an athlete. Sure, she could swim. But she was more at home in a pool than the sea. The alternative was mind-blowing, meaningless sex. The sex sounded so much better than surfing, but a girl had to have some standards.

"Okay, let's do it," she said. Then she winced.

Alex just laughed. A loud, booming sound that melded perfectly with the pounding surf.

Relieved that he didn't seem to hold her hesitation against

her, Dru picked up the surfboard he indicated. It was too wide to fit under her arm the way he carried his, so she followed his instructions and—feeling more clumsy than sexy—carried it balanced on her head.

"Wouldn't this be better earlier in the day?" she asked, struggling to balance the board while her feet sank into the shifting sands as she followed him down to the shore.

"Nah, this is the perfect time. Everyone is still at siesta, so it's quiet. Besides, I have the feeling you'll be a quick study. We'll get through the basics and I'll bet you're on the board by this evening. There's nothing like surfing at sunset."

"Like you were last night?" She gave him a curious glance, wondering at a life filled with such trouble-free pleasures. How did he stand the simplicity of it? Was that as much a part of his appeal as his gorgeous face and broad shoulders? That easygoing attitude so at odds with her own life. "Do you surf every sunset?"

"As many as I can," he admitted, glancing out at the Sea of Cortez with a look of pleasure on his face. Much as she'd stare at the stars in the night sky or a sexy man's naked body. Joyous, contented appreciation.

Dru wanted to feel that. That simple confidence evidenced in Alex's look. As if he saw the challenges and not only accepted them but longed to meet them head-on. But most of all, that he knew perfectly well he was up to whatever came his way.

For a woman who had to give herself pep talks on a daily basis, that look was like a drug she craved.

Then he shifted his attention, studying her. The warm appreciation remained in his eyes, along with a healthy dose of lusty interest. Dru had never had anyone look at her like that. As if the idea of being with her made him happy, horny and amused all at the same time.

And that was even more tempting than the confidence he showed facing the surf's wild challenge.

Suddenly determined to somehow capture both Alex's confidence and his admiration, she drew her shoulders back and lifted her chin for the last three steps through the sand.

When they reached the water's edge, he indicated that she should attach the leg leash to her left foot. Then she lifted the board again and followed him into the sea.

Dru gasped at the chill of the water compared to the warmth of the beach. Alongside Alex, she waded out until the water reached her hips, then, trying to mimic his easy movement, pulled herself onto the surfboard.

"Let's paddle out past the first break," he told her, his voice just under a shout to be heard over the crashing of the waves. "Remember how I told you to cup your hands? Like you're swimming."

Swimming was a lot easier, Dru decided after a couple of minutes. Belly flat on the board, she struggled against the waves pushing her one way while the undertow tugged her another. She eyed the round, rock-hard muscles of Alex's biceps as he paddled, and realized that he probably didn't have to use weights for his fantastic physique.

Her arms burning, Dru kept her eyes on him, squinting against the spray of salt water peppering her face. Like the pot of gold at the end of the rainbow, he was her reward for the suffering her body was now experiencing. Maybe she should have spent more time talking to him before going along with this mad surfing idea. They had to have some area of common interest.

A wave slapped her in the face, making her gasp at the sting. Breathing and walking upright were better common ground than this, she decided with a low growl.

"Here's good," Alex called to her over his shoulder. He

shifted, pushing up into a sitting position to straddle the board. "C'mon up."

Abandoning any semblance of grace or even strength, Dru wiggled until she was straddling her board, too.

"You're like those people who run marathons for entertainment, aren't you?" she accused.

His grin flashed, but Alex shook his head. "Nah. I've never been much into group events. The idea of someone slapping a number on my chest and telling me what direction to aim my feet holds no appeal."

Now that she wasn't paddling her ass off, Dru was able to catch her breath and look around. Her chest was still heaving from the exertion, but she was blown away at the beauty of the view. Water, everywhere. Brilliant blue, fading to pale white where it washed up on the deep gold sand of the beach. All around, the water seemed to blend into the sky. It felt as if she were being held on the edge of heaven. Despite her labored breath and screaming muscles, a sense of peace washed over her.

"It's amazing out here," she said softly.

"You get it," he said, his tone low but delighted. As if talking too loudly would desecrate the serenity of the moment. "No matter what is going on in my life, when I come out here, I know I can deal with it."

Dru tilted her head, blinking against the sun reflecting off the water. "The sea gives you strength?"

"In a way." His tone was contemplative, and he looked out at the water as he might a lover. "More like I realize out here that so much is beyond my control. It lets me see how unimportant some things are, and how vital others might be."

Then, as if he were shaking the water out of his hair, he tossed off the philosophical mantle that was starting to fascinate Dru and glanced over his shoulder.

"And then there's the whole man versus nature thing, too," he said with a grin, nodding to indicate the wave building behind them. "Once you get the hang of being one with the ocean, you know how strong you are."

Dru followed his gaze, her eyes going huge and her stomach diving down to Davy Jones's locker. She gulped, wondering if she could ride the wave belly down. It was bound to hurt less.

"Remember what I taught you," Alex said, already flattening his body on the board. His toes were tucked under, his hands gripping the sides of the board. "Paddle with the wave until you feel it build, then push up to your feet and squat. Keep your knees loose, focus on your core."

Ever the good student, Dru followed his directions. As if her biceps and shoulders weren't still aching from her earlier abuse, she paddled like hell, feeling the water swell beneath the board.

Half terrified, half numb, she watched Alex and mimicked his moves. As the wave built, she grabbed the sides of her board. Her heart pounding, she pushed up and tugged her feet beneath her as if she was doing a jumping-jack push-up. She pried her fingers from the board and stood, knees bent, arms outstretched for balance.

Already riding the wave, Alex glanced over to make sure she was okay. He shot her a huge smile and a thumbs-up.

A satisfied kind of lust settled in Dru's churning stomach. Yes. She'd done it. In that moment, for one brief second, she knew she could handle anything life threw her way.

Thirty minutes later, Dru followed Alex's directions and headed for the beach. She reached the shore and unhooked the tether from her ankle before rolling off the board.

The most incredible energy coursed through her body, filling her with an excitement and freedom like she'd never felt before. Unable to lift the board in her quivering arms, she dragged it out of the water with her. Breathless, she clambered up the beach. She only made it about ten steps toward the Surf Shack and couldn't resist any longer. She plunged the board into the sand. Then she threw her arms out as if to embrace the magic of the experience and turned in a circle with a laugh.

"Oh, my God," she breathed. "That's like heaven."

Talk about exhilarating. It was the best sex she'd ever had, a chocolate binge and the view from the top of the Grand Canyon all rolled into one fabulous surge of delight. She watched Alex stride out of the sea, looking once again like a modern-day water god.

The laughter still dancing on her lips, her breath hitched at the intensity in his eyes. He wasn't laughing with her. He was staring at her as if she was the most incredible sight he'd ever seen. The edible kind, as if he was starving and had to take a bite. Her smile fell away, her chest rising and falling with her quick breaths.

He didn't even bother to stick his board in the sand. He just tossed it aside and strode forward. Dru's heart tumbled over itself, it was racing so fast. Heat flared deep in her belly, so hot she wondered why her wet swimsuit wasn't steaming.

He stopped a few inches away. Close enough for her to smell the sea overlaying his own rich, masculine scent. His hair hung in wet curls around his face, droplets of water trailing down his throat. Over his collarbone. Onto his chest. Her mouth watered. She wanted to trace that water with her tongue. Would it taste salty like the sea? Or would she taste him?

She had to know.

Just as she took a step forward, Alex reached out and cupped his hands on either side of her head. Dru's body melted at the powerful move, her nipples beading in supplication against the tight, wet fabric of her swimsuit. He tilted her head back. His body pressed into hers, his arousal hard and obvious behind the wet cotton of his trunks as it pushed against her belly.

Before she could do more than register a surprised *oh* of pleasure at how hard and long he felt, his mouth took hers.

It was like surfing. Exhilarating, dangerous, addictive. His lips slid, soft and sweet, over hers. He molded her mouth gently before his tongue traced her bottom lip. She gave a sigh at how perfect it all felt.

Then he shifted. She had no idea how, but the kiss went from mellow to incendiary with just the brush of his tongue. Everything changed. She felt her world tilt, a sideways slide into a dark, intense well of pleasure. Her arms hung useless at her sides, her head dropping back in his hands, giving over total control. Helpless to do anything but enjoy, she let the passion engulf her.

ALEX HAD NEVER BELIEVED he'd find anything that enthralled him as much as the sea. Until Drucilla. Sexy, sweet and oh, God, he thought as he deepened the kiss, so freaking delicious.

Fingers tunneled through her hair, all loose and wet where it escaped its tidy braid, he held her head captive for his mouth. Teeth, tongue and breath tangled together in a wild dance of passion. His heart beat as if he was riding the highest wave; his body responded as if the touch of her mouth had flipped his switch, turning him on at full power.

Her lips tasted like salt, sun and something indefinable. Something that reached into his heart and tugged. A lesser man might have hesitated, worried that a woman he'd known less than twenty-four hours could capture him so tightly, so quickly. But Alex knew better—there was no such thing as love. Appreciation, enjoyment, respect, definitely. And sexual connection? His body's reaction to Drucilla proved how intense those could be. But love? Pretty words was all.

Positive his heart was safe, Alex gave over to the delight he was discovering in this fascinating woman.

Her arms twined around his neck, a low purr of pleasure husky in her throat. She moved tight against his body, her smooth thighs sliding along his. Alex hummed in appreciation. Drucilla hadn't lied when she'd said she wasn't into games. No, this woman went for what she wanted. And from the way her hands were skimming over his arms, gripping his biceps, she wanted him.

Their mouths moved together, each slide of their lips sending him into a deeper chasm of gratification. He shifted his weight, sinking to the sand and bringing Dru with him.

She made a sound of approval, then scraped her nails lightly over his chest. Alex groaned, pleasure shooting through his body, sending his senses to high alert. Propping himself on one elbow, he deepened the kiss as he used the other hand to trace her swimsuit strap. His fingers trailed down the silken skin of her shoulder, across the delicate curve of her collarbone. Unable to resist the temptation, he cupped his palm over the swell of her breast, which was straining against the slick, wet nylon of her swimsuit.

She gasped, her back arching to press herself tighter into his hand. Alex moaned, the feel of her nipple swelling beneath making him crazy.

Dimly, the far-off voice of reason reminded him that for all their seeming seclusion, they were on a public beach. And from the feel of the sun against his shoulder blades, siesta was probably over. Which meant this beach was about to get even more public.

Definitely not how or where he wanted to enjoy his first sight of Drucilla's naked body. Oh, no, when he got her naked he wanted all the time in the world to enjoy every nuance of her body, to revel in the colors and textures and tastes of her.

A part of him wanted to haul her to her feet and drag her off to the nearest private spot and give in to his body's demands. But he couldn't. Well, he acknowledged as his erection throbbed in painful protest, he could. But he wouldn't.

Forcing himself to be patient was about the hardest thing Alex had ever done. Almost as hard as his dick, pressing in supplication against Drucilla's thigh. But he wanted more than a hot dance in the sand with her. He wanted as much as he could get.

"How about we clean up, go to dinner?" he asked, his words husky and rough. "Maybe some dancing later?"

She blinked up at him, her indigo eyes shifting from blurry to contemplative. She was shaded from the glare of the late-afternoon sun by his shadow, but the light still glinted off the water sparkling on her lush eyelashes.

She opened her mouth to respond, then pursed her lips, scanning his face as if looking for the answer to the mysteries of the universe. Then she gave a deep sigh. Alex almost groaned as the move pressed her breasts, with their rock-hard nipples, against his chest.

"How about we skip the dinner and dancing and just go back to my bungalow?" she invited softly. Her words were breathless, nervous. But the assurance in her eyes told him she meant what she said.

Alex's mind exploded with the image of the two of them, naked beneath a shower's spray, sliding their soapy hands over each other's bodies to wash away the salt and sand.

His dick, already straining and impatient, jumped a little at the mental picture. His mind, already formulating an acceptance, thrilled at the invitation.

But his mouth, dammit, was operating on its own.

"Let's do both," he said before he could stop the words.

His mind immediately scrambled to find a way to retract the words.

Drucilla's eyes went soft, something sweet and humbling flashing in their depths. It was that look that instantly put an end to any attempted retraction.

Alex gave a soft laugh and rested his forehead against hers, briefly closing his eyes and sucking in a deep, fortifying breath. God, he was known for his mental acuity, his brilliance, some even said. And here he was turning his back on loose-and-wild sex in exchange for a more meaningful connection.

Insane.

"Let's do dinner," he suggested, reluctantly pulling away from her warmth. Instantly chilled now that his still-wet body was exposed to the air, he shivered a little as he pushed himself to his feet. Reaching down, he took her hand to help her up.

The momentum of the move had the exact effect he'd hoped. She landed against him. Alex's arms wrapped around her, his erection tight against her belly. He grinned down into her inquiring face.

"We'll save the dancing for private."

4

DRU WATCHED HERSELF in the mirror as she tied the satin strings of her halter behind her neck. The teal-and-amethyst-patterned fabric made her skin glow. Or maybe that was the sun she'd gotten that afternoon. The smooth material cupped her breasts, making it clear she wasn't wearing a bra.

She stepped back to get a full-length view, turning this way and that to see if her panty line showed. Barely. That was good, wasn't it? She knew the underwear rules at home. Wear it. Simple enough. But vacation-underwear rules? And what about the wanting-to-have-sex-tonight rule modification?

She expected the lack of a bra would clearly indicate her interest in sex. But she wasn't quite brave enough to go commando, so she hoped her barely there panty line wouldn't be a turnoff.

This, she realized, was why she sucked at the flirtation thing. She obsessed over trivial details. She didn't know the rules, the right way to play the game. She smoothed her hand over her hip and gave a ragged sigh. What she wouldn't give to discuss interstellar gases and dust clouds at this point.

It wasn't until she went to twist her hair into a knot that she noticed her hands were shaking. Dru looked at her reflection, noting the dilated eyes beneath her smoky shadow, the bare lower lip where she'd already chewed off her lipstick and the rapid pulse fluttering at her throat.

She dropped her hands, letting her hair fall like a pale curtain over her shoulders. She'd leave it down. The better to hide behind, she hoped.

She glanced at the clock: 5:55. Alex would be here in five minutes. Resorting to her test-anxiety cure, she picked up her brush and started running it through her hair. She closed her eyes and focused on the sensation of the bristles, on her breath moving gently in and out. She let her mind empty. Drew in relaxation and a sense of peace.

The tension seeped out of her shoulders. The butterflies in her stomach landed. Ahhh, there it was. That sweet sense of tranquillity. Perfect.

There was a knock at the door. Dru gave a loud gasp. The brush flew out of her hands, ricocheted off the mirror and slid across the bureau with a loud bang.

Apparently she couldn't have both inner peace and a wild vacation fling. She sucked in a shaky breath before quickly slicking color back over her lower lip with a quivering hand. With a smacking motion, she blew her reflection a kiss for luck and headed for the door.

She pressed a hand to her stomach. Then, with a deep breath, she pasted a smile on her face and pulled open the door.

"Hi," she said breathlessly.

"Hi back."

Oh, baby. Alex was gorgeous. So far she'd only seen his hair in wet curls or casual waves falling around his face. Tonight it was swept back in a way that accented his cheekbones and emphasized his melt-her-insides midnight-dark eyes.

His white shirt was open at the collar and buttoned at the cuffs, paired with black slacks and dress shoes. Typical date attire, evening casual. The look should have been staid, maybe a little cookie-cutter.

Maybe it was the intense, edgy lust clawing at her belly that had her wondering how the crisp white cotton would feel under her hands if she stroked his chest. How the zipper would feel as she tugged it down. If his clothes carried the same delicious scent she'd smelled on his skin when they'd kissed that afternoon.

Whether he wore boxers or briefs.

Her anxiety melted away in the heat of pure lust.

"Wow," he said, his tone husky as he leaned his shoulder against the door frame and gave her a slow, seductive smile. The kind of smile that promised that he could deliver on her every fantasy. "You look gorgeous."

"Come in," she invited, her mind racing with possibilities. Her brain was disengaged, all her earlier concerns over common ground disintegrated. Who needed similar interests to talk about? All she could think about now was sex. With Alex. To have that, she just needed a simple plan. Entice him, entertain him, engage him.

In other words, get him naked as quickly as possible.

He stepped into the room, shutting the door behind him. As he did, he handed her a single bloom. Brilliant red, it was huge and fragrant. And so, so sweet.

"Thank you," she murmured softly.

Dru took the lily, her hands brushing Alex's as her eyes met his. Her heart stuttered. No guy had ever brought her flowers. Once in a while one would bring her a science journal, but only if they had an article featured in it.

"I love flowers," she blurted out as she held the fragrant blossom to her nose with a smile. "My mom does a lot of container gardening, but she's always grown herbs and vegetables, never flowers."

Alex followed her to the small living room and, at her

gesture, sat on the cushioned rattan settee while Dru found a glass at the wet bar and filled it with water for the flower.

"Wine?" she asked, lifting the bottle she'd put on ice. Just in case.

"Sure."

She pulled the cork and poured them both a glass, and was proud to see her hand was steady.

"Does your mom live in an apartment?" he asked with a friendly smile.

Dru almost dropped her wine. Olympia Robichoux, in an apartment? With all those other people around, sharing walls and noise? Hardly. Olympia had always insisted on a house, no matter what their financial situation. A house was more regal, she said. That they were easier to sneak out of went without saying. Shrugging off the tension that thoughts of her mother always induced, Dru handed Alex his wine before taking a fortifying sip of her own.

"No. My parents just moved a lot," she told him as she settled next to him on the settee. It sounded better than sharing her family's eviction records. As always, she stuffed the childhood anger, resentment and dregs of loneliness away in a tidy little box in her mind labeled "off-limits." "My mother kept everything she needed portable. But my dad wanted his fresh tomatoes, so he had to lug those huge clay pots with them from house to house."

"Is he still lugging them?"

"My dad's gone," she said with a smile to acknowledge the sympathetic way he rubbed her knee. "Mom bought a house three years ago, so her gypsy days are over."

Well, technically, she'd helped her mom buy the house. It'd been crazy, given that she'd just bought her own condo. But her mom had needed a home. One she could actually settle in and trust would never be torn out from under her.

The choice had been to buy one or move Olympia into the condo.

That decision had been a no-brainer.

And she didn't expect gratitude. She really didn't. But someday, dammit, her mom would actually plant something in the ground instead of those clay pots.

"Gypsy days, huh?" Said in that deep, sexy tone, Alex made the idea sound intriguing. Almost sexy and adventurous instead of pathetic and lonely. "That sounds like an interesting childhood."

"It does sound that way, hmm."

He gave her a long look. The kind that said he could see through her skin and into her heart. "And what about you? What was your preference?"

His tone, soft with just a hint of concern, told her she'd given too much away. This was supposed to be a sexy adventure, not some quick trip through her battered psyche. So she just smiled and forced her shoulders to relax.

"I have to admit, I'm partial to fresh tomatoes, too."

"Ah, a daddy's girl?"

A familiar pain stabbed through her, making Dru wince. Daddy's girl. She'd heard that phrase so often growing up. From her father, it was in a tone of pride that his little girl was so good at the science he loved and could make a career of which he'd only dreamed. From her mother, it was usually preceded by, "Did you have to be just like him?"

No. She wasn't letting it be an issue. Not here. Not now. Instead, Dru shook her head and sipped her wine before saying, "I'm hardly a girl."

"No," he conceded, lifting his hand. Dru held her breath as he reached for her. Her heart raced as she wondered where he'd touch her. It settled into a fast gallop as he rubbed the ends of her hair between his fingers. The back of his hand was inches away from her breast, the warmth of him heating her nipple into an aware kind of craving. She wanted to breathe deeply, to push herself against his hand. At the same time, she wanted him to make the move. To want her enough to push past the first-date etiquette and get right to the hot sex.

As if he read her mind, Alex grinned. That wicked, naughty tilt of his lips that said he knew every sexy thought in her head and planned to make each one a reality. In his own good time.

Right now, he wanted to get to know her better.

Still playing with her hair, he said, "You're definitely all woman. The kind of woman who calls her own shots, who knows what she wants and goes for it. Like tomatoes." He grinned and raised a brow as his fingers left her hair to trace a gentle design over her bare shoulder. "Do you grow your own tomatoes, too? Or does your mom keep you supplied?"

"I've got a black thumb," she admitted, barely focusing on the discussion. Most of her attention was on his finger and the ever-widening pattern he was searing into her sensitive flesh. "My mom gives me a basket each week when I stop by to take care of things for her. You know, some yard work, some errands, some chores around the house. I'll have half a bushel waiting when I get home."

"Is your mom older?"

"No," she said with a shrug that brought his hand even closer to the edge of her bodice. Excitement spun tighter through her system, and her entire being was focused on that hand, her nipple, all the possibilities. "She's in her fifties."

"Is she disabled?" he asked, his tone as distracted as her thoughts.

His hand was now tracing the silky strap of her halter. Up her throat. Down her chest. Up along her shoulder. Down toward her breast. Dru breathed more shallowly, not wanting to do anything to impede his movements.

"Hardly," she murmured, barely tracking their conversation.

"She's healthy as a horse. She just sort of lives in her own little world and forgets things. You know, like paying bills, mowing the lawn, picking up the cleaning."

"So you do it for her?" The smile he gave her was like a spark that lit the fuse of passion in her belly. Deep, intense desire warmed and spread, causing a damp heat to pool between her legs.

"Someone has to. I—" She stopped and frowned, realizing what he'd said. And what she'd admitted.

How did he do that? Dru shifted just a little on the settee, trying to hide her discomfort. She didn't like talking about her family. Hadn't she changed the subject? Weren't they supposed to be focused on sexy stuff instead?

As if sensing her withdrawal, he dropped his hand to the seat between them and gave her an inquiring look.

"How about you?" she countered desperately. "Is your family local?"

She winced as soon as the words left her lips. Dumb question. Alex himself was obviously not local, even if he did work here.

"We, well, my mom has an apartment in Cabo," Alex said, surprising her. She scanned his face, seeing an amused sort of resignation in his dark eyes. "Like your parents, she's into the gypsy lifestyle. One way or another, though, we always ended up here at least once a year. So she keeps a place in town, mostly for show. I think having a home base makes her feel a little more settled."

"Is that where you're staying?" she asked, trying to be subtle about prying into his private life. Was a guy who lived at his mother's—even if his mother was rarely there—considered a momma's boy? *It doesn't matter,* she reminded herself. *Alex is playmate material, he doesn't need hang-on-to-for-life potential.*

"Nah, she sublet it to a couple from Montana for the month.

I'm never sure when I'm going to be here, and she's never sure where she wants to be, so it's easier if I stay at the hotel."

Definitely not a momma's boy.

"Doesn't that bother you?" Dru asked, knowing such a nebulous relationship would drive her crazy. As crazy as her frustratingly codependent relationship with her own mother? Was that possible? She wished she could ask him how he dealt with it. Whether he blamed himself.

It was hard to think, though. He was so close. For the first time in her life, her brain wasn't functioning.

Who knew that could be so sexy?

"Bother me? Nah," he said absently. His eyes traced a path over her face, down her throat and across the swell of her breasts. Like a warm caress, she felt their touch deep in her belly.

"So what do you do for a living?" he asked, clearly trying to steer the conversation back to safe ground.

Well, there ya go, he'd found her one surefire passion douser. Dru stared wide-eyed at this sexy, gorgeous man looking at her as if she was a wet dream, and imagined telling him she had a Ph.D. in astrophysics.

Oh, no, not going there, she promised herself. For this vacation, for this man, she was going to be just a woman. Not a scientist, not a shy geek and definitely not a sexual failure. This was all about the fantasy.

"You know, it's vacation time," she said quietly, taking a chance and running her finger along his thigh. "I'd rather not talk work, do you mind?"

He smiled slowly, then his gaze dropped to her bodice again. Her skin heated under his appraisal. He lifted his hand off the seat between them, rubbing the fabric of her skirt between his fingers in tactile appreciation.

"Nobody's ever looked at me like you do," she blurted. As soon as the words escaped, Dru wanted to grab them back.

Eyes huge, she pressed her lips together and winced, waiting for his reaction.

Alex laughed. A deep, husky laugh that made her think of moonlit nights and silk sheets.

"I like looking at you. You remind me of a fairy princess. Not the cartoon kind. The kind with ancient magic. A very sexy, very intriguing magical fairy princess," he said, that seductive smile of his still playing over his lips.

Dru couldn't tell what heated faster, her heart or her body. Suddenly everything was a molten puddle of gooey lust. Who knew a man could seduce her with the simplest touch, the sweetest words?

Unable to stop herself, barely hearing the warning in her head to let him make the first move, Dru leaned forward. Desire flamed in his dark eyes, the sparks warning her she was so far out of her element that she might not find her way back.

But she couldn't stop. As if in slow motion, she rubbed her lips over his. Soft. Oh, so soft.

She started to pull back, but his gaze held hers captive.

She couldn't move. She could barely breathe. Her heart, pounding louder than the sea itself, lodged in her throat.

Then he shifted. The tiniest fraction was all it took for him to seize control. Sure he could do a better job than her, she gladly let him take charge.

Smooth and tender, his lips danced over hers. Sliding in a sweet caress, the kiss was straight out of one of those fairy tales he'd spoken of. Oh, yeah, he was so much better at this than she was. Reveling in the sensations flashing through her system like a meteor shower, Dru hummed low in her throat.

He growled in return, shifting again. The kiss went from sweetly seductive to intensely erotic. One hand slid from her shoulders to her waist, gripping her tighter. The other plunged through the heavy curtain of her hair to curve over the back of her neck and pull her closer.

His tongue slipped, hot and wet, over the seam of her lips. He didn't ask for entry, he demanded it. Dru's mind spun out of orbit as he claimed her. As the shimmering heat poured through her veins, she swore she felt her brain cells actually explode in lust.

His kiss was an erotic invitation, tongue and lips seducing her. Her pulse raced and her stomach zinged. When he scraped his teeth over her sensitive lower lip, a shudder went through her, and her nipples contracted to tight, hard buds. She wished he'd touch her, stroke the aching flesh.

Dru leaned closer in unspoken invitation.

Alex slowly pulled his lips from hers. She would have moaned in protest, but she'd lost her voice.

He took a deep breath, his face as calm as ever.

Disappointment crashed over her, slapping at her confidence, mocking her desire. She was so easily set aside without her brainy persona. Albert Einstein's face flashed through her mind, taunting that even her brainy self was easily set aside. The feminine assurance that'd urged her to pursue Alex, always a shaky thing for her, crashed.

So much for having herself a fling.

If the man could kiss her into a wet, crazy puddle of passionate longing, then set her aside with a calm smile, she was obviously out of her league. She'd be better off with the gasper. Or even the wheezer.

Then she saw the wild racing pulse in his throat. Her eyes dropped to look at their fingers, twined together on the seat, but before she did more than note how tanned he was compared to her, her gaze locked on the huge tented bulge in his slacks.

Well, well. She definitely wasn't the only one affected, it seemed. Her shaky confidence solidified, shooting sky high.

"We should go," Alex said as he raised their entwined fingers, brushing his knuckles along her jawline. "Our reservations are in a few minutes."

Drucilla met his eyes, noting the sexual heat still lurking in their dark depths. She licked her lips. His eyes narrowed. She moved, just a smidge, closer. He swallowed.

She drew in a shaky breath. And she decided.

"Why don't we skip dinner," she said as she slipped her fingers from his and wrapped her arms around his neck. She gave him a tiny, hopefully seductive smile and pulled his head down to hers. Millimeters away from the delicious delight of his lips, she whispered, "We can start with dessert instead."

AS HER LIPS MOVED over his, shock rocked his system. Not only because of her invitation, although that was making his mind spin. But at her kiss. This definitely wasn't a bashful kiss.

God, he couldn't wait to get her naked. The world would tilt off its axis. Did she like it gentle and slow? Or would she let herself go? He'd seen her in a bikini, knew her body was long and slender. But he wanted—needed—to see her naked. To test the weight of her breasts. To see the color of her nipples, pressing so delicately against the silken fabric of her dress.

Torturing himself, he pulled his lips away to trace kisses along her cheek, over her jaw. He leaned closer to breathe in her fragrance. Soft and light, it reminded him of warm spring nights in a garden. It was all he could do not to bury his face in her soft silvery curtain of hair and see if her scent was stronger there.

His body ached. His fingers tingled. He needed to touch her. To taste her. To feel her body as she exploded for him. He wanted to strip her naked so he could taste that smooth skin, kissed pale gold by a day in the sun.

His dick, straining for attention, was a throbbing reminder of just how exciting she was. But taking her to bed before he'd even taken her to dinner just seemed…hot. Sexy. Wildly tempting.

And pushy.

Only a jerk got pushy with a fairy princess.

He leaned back and gave her a shaky smile.

"Don't you know it's bad to have dessert first?" he forced himself to offer, his voice as tight as his body.

When the hell he'd turned into such a gentleman, he had no idea. But he couldn't yank the words back, so he forced a patient smile onto his face and prepared to talk his dick down.

Her eyes, so expressive, flashed. First confusion, then irritation, then determination. Alex realized that for all her ethereal looks, Drucilla wasn't a woman to be condescended to.

Nor was she a quick fling, someone to do on the first date. Regardless about his feelings toward commitment, he'd never been a one-night kind of guy. And after just one day, he had the feeling he was going to want to see a lot more of Drucilla. Quite a lot more.

He'd called her a fairy princess. Pure sexual fantasy was more like it. He was completely and totally rock hard. From just a kiss. A fully clothed, no groping, simple kiss.

And now he was putting a halt to things.

God, he was an idiot.

"You're right. Dessert first is bad," Drucilla agreed, scattering his thoughts all to hell and back when she slid her hand up his chest so that he felt each and every finger's caress through the thin fabric of his shirt.

She leaned closer and brushed her lips over his again, leaving fiery tingles as she pulled back and gave him a seductive look through her lashes.

"But for once," she told him quietly, "I'd love to see how bad I can be."

5

ALEX'S MIND WENT NUMB while his dick went hard. Harder? Even harder than before, if that was possible.

"Bad?" he asked, even as he ran his hands over the warm curve of her shoulders and down her spine. In a quick, easy move he had her sitting across his lap. She gave a breathless giggle and linked her own hands behind his neck again to steady herself.

"Bad," she repeated. Tilting her chin to meet his kiss, she whispered against his mouth, "As bad as I could possibly be."

Breath hitching a little at her words, he thought of all the ways he'd like to be bad with her. A couple involved toys, one included hot oil and a rubber mat and, for a second, his mouth watered at the idea of leather restraints.

Then he blinked, focusing on Drucilla again. Sweet, ethereal and hardly up for his kinkier fantasies. But the rest of his fantasies? His finger traced the pale, gentle curve of her cheekbone, skimming over the sharp edge of her jaw to trace a path down her swanlike throat.

Her soft sigh verged on a purr.

Oh, yeah, she was pure fantasy material. Of the sweetest

kind, actually. And from the look on her face, he was starring front and center in a few of her fantasies, too.

Despite the waves of passion pounding over him, Alex had to smile at the earnest lust shining in her eyes. Two emotions he'd never have put together. It made him feel like a super-hero, a sexual guru whose knowledge she was desperately eager to partake of.

And, hey, if she was willing to climb the mountain, who was he to deny her his pearls of wisdom. In moderation, of course. He didn't want to scare her.

Eager to fulfill both of their cravings, he swept his lips over hers. She tasted like wine. But beneath the essence of grapes was something darker, something intensely delicious. Something he couldn't resist.

Alex slid into the kiss with pleasure. Tracing his tongue over the fullness of her bottom lip, he reveled in the texture of her mouth, in the softness of her tongue as it danced lightly against his.

She was delicious. He could feel just the hint of hesitation in her, as if she didn't have a lot of experience. Warning himself again not to rush her, he became lost in her flavor.

It wasn't until he felt the tight bud of her nipple nudging his palm that he realized he'd curved his hand over her breast. That's how entranced he was by the magic of her mouth. But now that his hand had kicked a signal to his brain, he widened his focus.

Small enough to do justice to going braless, but generous enough to fill his cupped palm perfectly, her breast pressed against the flowery silk.

Before he could do more than wish he could see what was beneath the fabric, her hand slid under her curtain of hair and with a couple flicks of her fingers, the material sagged beneath his palm.

"One of your bad-girl moves?" he teased, pleased to see his words chase away the shadowy nerves from her eyes.

"Care to counter it with a bad-boy response?" she teased right back, a tiny smile playing at the edges of that sexy mouth.

A hundred responses, only a few verbal, crowded Alex's mind. Enjoying the anticipation, he held her gaze with his as, with one hand still cupping her breast through the silk, he reached up to trail the other along the loosened, gaping fabric. He saw the expectation in her eyes, felt her chest rise as she sucked in a quick breath.

But he was going slow here. So instead of pulling her dress free, he leaned forward to press a wet, openmouthed kiss against the silk.

She gasped, her hand lifting to his head to keep him from moving back. He liked that. Liked that she was willing to let him know what she wanted.

It boded well for the rest of their little adventure.

He wet the fabric with damp heat while softly kneading her other breast through the silk. Using his teeth, he scraped the fabric. She gasped in approval and curled her fingers into his hair.

Taking her cue from him, Drucilla used the hand that wasn't holding his head to draw her fingernails gently over his shoulders, then down his chest, grazing his nipple. Pleasure speared through Alex straight to his dick.

Needing more, he pulled the straps free and let the brightly colored fabric fall.

He leaned back so he could see all of her all at once. Her hand clutched his hair for a brief second before she let go and, with a shaky breath, watched him take in the sight.

Slender shoulders and lightly muscled arms framed her chest, the gentle sweep of her upturned breasts tipped with the sweetest shade of pink. He watched as they tightened even more under his hot gaze and he smiled. She was perfect.

Her nipples were so sensitive. He reached out to rub his knuckle over one, then the other, his body tightening at the swift, intense response. They puckered and pouted at the lightest touch. With hooded eyes, he watched his fingers, so tan against the alabaster of her breasts, swirl an ever-tightening pattern around her delicately budding areola.

She reached out and made quick work of the buttons on his shirt. Wanting those hands on him, Alex helped her by tugging the material free of his belt, unbuttoning from the bottom up. Their busy hands met at his belly button, fingers tangling.

He was prepared for the pleasure of her hand on his chest, the feel of her probably curious and possibly a little shy exploration of his body. He wasn't prepared for her to bypass the now-bared skin and head straight for his lap. Her fingers cupped the length of him through his slacks, testing the weight of his erection.

Oh, yeah, baby, he almost groaned. He grew obligingly heavier. A guy had to be grateful for a compliant dick.

He leaned forward to suck her nipple into his mouth. Her gasp turned to a moan, letting him know he'd found one of her hot buttons.

He tormented them both by working the stiff peak with his tongue and teeth as he slid his free hand along her calf. He was pretty sure he'd have kept it there, below her knee, if Drucilla hadn't wiggled her butt against his lap, the tiny undulations keeping beat with her panting little moans.

What was a guy to do but slide his hand higher? Her thighs were pressed together, but at his fingers' silent entreaty, her knees loosened in welcome.

Alex almost gave a panting little moan of his own.

He knew from their surf date that her thighs were firm and softly muscled. Yoga thighs, he figured. Slender, strong, sleek.

And hot.

His fingers trailed under her skirt. Teasing little forays between the silken fabric and equally silky flesh.

She gently scraped her nails over his shoulders again, then curled her hands around his biceps with a growl of appreciation. The move, the sound, made him feel huge and strong and, well, so freaking manly.

Drucilla gave a throaty moan and pressed her thighs tight, capturing his hand. Obviously not to stop him, though, since she lifted her hips to give him better access.

Needing to see her, to watch her reactions, Alex lifted his head to stare into her eyes. Drucilla stared right back, her eyes blurred with desire. Not breaking the stare, she dropped her head against the back of the couch and shifted her hips in invitation.

Her eyes closed and she moaned. Long, breathy moans. Her panting intensified as his fingers slipped in and out, faster and harder. He slid his thumb along her damp, passion-swollen flesh and her moans turned to gasps. Her hips moved faster and, her eyes still locked on his, she slipped over the edge with a keening little cry of delight.

Alex watched her eyelids flutter, then she let her head fall back as tiny after-tremors rocked through her.

God, he felt huge. And not just behind the zipper. Alex slipped his fingers free, wrapped both arms around her slender shoulders and pulled her against his chest.

He drew in a deep breath and figured a few more and he might have enough control to stand without breaking anything vital. Then he'd escort her to dinner, show her a great time and hopefully, after they shared some sweet chocolate empanadas, they'd return here for round two.

A round he figured he'd enjoy twice as much.

Knowing control would be impossible with her half-naked on his lap, Alex moved to shift Drucilla aside. She made a sound of protest and tightened her arms.

"Bed," she finally suggested, the words barely a breath against his throat.

Alex's body stiffened even more—an almost impossible feat, he'd have thought. Here he'd been hoping to work his way up to an admission to a great time, and she was offering him an all-access pass to heaven. A thrill ride to paradise. One he wanted only as much as he wanted his next breath. So why was he hesitating?

Alex pulled back enough to gaze at Drucilla's face. He noted the glistening temptation of her swollen lips, parted just enough to make him want to dive back in. Her hair tumbled like a silken cloud around her face. But it was her eyes, those slumberous blue depths, that tugged at him. That sent every thought, every stupid doubt, right out the window.

Not bothering to retie her halter, he lifted her in his arms, pressing a hot, openmouthed kiss to the straining nipple closest to him before striding toward the bedroom. At her door, he gently set her on her feet. The moonlight shimmered, filling the room with a surreal glow.

His eyes locked on hers, he leaned down to take her mouth. Just the softest whisper of his lips over hers as he skimmed the pad of his fingers over the berry-soft tips of her breasts.

She tugged at his shirt, shoving the fabric off his arms and letting it drop to the ground. Her hands were like fire, rushing over his skin. She curved her fingers into the small of his back and pressed her breasts against his chest then rubbed them lightly so her nipples scored trails of heat across his flesh.

Alex dropped to his knees in front of her, ready to offer up homage to the delight that was her body.

"You're gorgeous," he told her as he gazed up the length of her. Then he prepared to drive her insane with desire.

SENSATIONS PULSED through Dru's body, tangling and twisting until she couldn't focus. Couldn't think. Could only feel.

Alex's mouth was hot and wet, trailing kisses over her stomach. Her knees went weak as his fingers unhooked her last bastion of modesty, the tiny hook holding her dress together at her hips. The fabric slid, soundless silk, down her legs into a soft puddle over her bare feet. He leaned back to get a good look.

This was her cue for shyness, but Dru couldn't find any. Instead, she reveled in the look in his dark, moonlit eyes. Passion, yes. A passion she was amazed to see. But more, there was appreciation in those midnight depths. And a promise.

A promise that told her she wouldn't wake up wondering if there wasn't something more. Because he'd make sure he showered her every possible ounce of pleasure two bodies could bring each other.

Her toes curled. Nerves or excitement, she wasn't sure. Didn't care. Empowered, whether it was from an odd lack of inhibition or the desperate need, she pressed her hand to the back of his head to invite him back to her aching body.

"Touch me," she whispered.

His grin was slow and sensual.

"Watch me," he demanded in return.

His fingers spread wide over her breasts, squeezing, then swirling so his palms grazed their aching peaks. She bit her lip and tunneled her fingers through his hair. His eyes held hers, demanding she stay with him. One hand still tweaked and tempted her nipple. But the other smoothed a long, tin-

gling path over her side to the scrap of satin-covered elastic
at her hip.

Dru heard the whimper of need before she realized she'd
made it.

She watched his finger until it slid out of sight. The sensation as it pressed teasingly against her G-spot almost made
her scream. He arched a brow as if to demand that she keep
watching, then, his own lids lowered as if in reverent prayer,
he leaned forward and ran his tongue along her wet slit.

Oh, God. His tongue was pure magic. She stared, her
vision blurring as he used his fingers and tongue to weave
a spell over her body. This was what sex was supposed to
be, she realized. Mind-numbing, body-shattering, intense
pleasure. And not a single Albert Einstein picture in sight.

Her thighs grew damp with the heat of his breath and
her own moisture. His finger worked her sensitive nub as
his tongue stabbed and swirled. Her belly tightened. Dru
gasped as the sensations coiled, tighter and tighter. After
that sweet little pop of an orgasm on the couch, she really
hadn't expected another one. At least, not without Alex, big
and naked, between her thighs.

Well, he was definitely between her thighs, although not
nearly naked enough. But oh, man, he was incredible. Her
legs started to shake. Her stomach clenched as she edged
closer to another orgasm, needy and suddenly desperate.

Breath coming in gasps now, she had to force herself not
to close her thighs to increase the pressure and hurry along
the building orgasm. Suffocating the man with the magic
tongue would put a quick end to what was promising to be
the most incredible night of her life.

He shifted, one hand kneading the soft flesh of her ass
while the other returned to tweak and torment her aching
nipple.

Then his tongue stabbed, once, twice and again. The

spring of passion exploded. Stars flashed behind her eyes and Dru gave a keening cry as the climax crashed over her in pounding, intense waves.

"You're incredible," she said with a soft smile, combing her fingers through the thick strands of his hair when he rose to wrap his arms around her.

"Ditto back at you," he teased.

"I want to make you feel as good as you do me." With that in mind, she reached down and flicked his belt open, then unhooked his slacks. Her fingers pressed against his straining erection before she slid the zipper down.

"We're not going to make it to the bed," he warned.

"Don't care," she panted, tugging at his slacks. "Now. Here. Fast."

He made a grab for his wallet, before he kicked the pants away, and pulled out a foil packet.

Should she tell him she was on birth control? Before she could, he'd ripped the packet open. Better safe anyway, she realized as she took the condom from him and fell to her knees so they were face-to-face.

Wanting—needing—to prove she was good enough to be worthy of a man as gorgeous, as incredible as Alex, Dru pressed her hand to his shoulders to indicate he should lie down on the carpet.

His grin flashed bright in the dark room. He leaned back, sweeping his hand along her thigh as he went.

Emboldened by the night, by Alex and the freedom of this entire adventure, Dru leaned forward to brush a soft, open-mouthed kiss over the velvety head of his straining dick.

He gave a breathless laugh and said, "Oh, no, you go there and we'll be at the cuddling segment of the evening much sooner than you'd probably like."

Thrilled that she might have the power to make him lose

control, Dru grinned and shifted so she could smooth the condom over the hard length of his cock.

"Talk to me," he said hoarsely. "Tell me what you want. Tell me what's next."

For the first time since they'd kissed on the couch, panic skittered up her spine. What should she say? Should she make something up? Use dirty words? Technical terms? God, she'd never talked dirty before.

She bit her lip and met his eyes. Seeing the edgy desire made her feel strong. But it was the calm appreciation there that doused the fear.

The guy had already given her two delicious orgasms. It wasn't as if she had anything to lose.

"I want you," she admitted as she smoothed her hand across the hard, tempting planes of his well-sculpted chest. She met his eyes, then forced herself to admit aloud, "I want to ride you. I need to feel you inside me. Deep, deep inside me."

He gave a guttural groan and tugged her up to meet his lips. Taking that as approval, Dru swung her leg over his and straddled his body. With a nervous swallow to wet her suddenly desert-dry throat, she lifted herself over his straining erection.

His eyes held hers, the pleasure and enjoyment in the dark depths encouraging her. Filling her with answering joy.

She sheathed him in one smooth, easy move.

Her breath rushed out in an ecstatic sigh and she started to move.

"Let me," he begged, his hands curving over the slight swell of her butt to gently lift, then lower her. Setting the rhythm of her ride with soft fingers and a warm smile.

He wanted to lead, she realized.

She gloried in the feel of him, so huge, so hard. He filled her, delighted her. She shifted, leaning down to lave one nipple before pressing kisses up his throat and taking his mouth in a wild, intense dance.

His fingers bit into her hips, an erotic ode to how much he wanted her. That he didn't miss a stroke, his rhythm still smooth and even, was a testament to his control.

Control she needed to make him lose, she realized. She needed to know she could.

With that in mind, Dru did the most difficult thing in her life. She completely shut off her thoughts and gave herself over to the sensations swirling between their bodies. She let herself be the sexy, wild woman she'd always dreamed of. She didn't know if she was more excited or more terrified.

She just knew she loved it.

Straightening, she captured his gaze and offered a slow smile. She ran her hands up her sides in a long, sinuous move, then cupped her own breasts as if they were offerings. His eyes narrowed to slits, but he didn't lose pace.

She swirled her index fingers around her already sensitized nipples. He hissed out a breath and tightened his grip. She moved her hands up her chest to her throat, then arched her back and lifted her arms, her fingers catching in the long, loose strands of her hair.

He moaned and released her. His hands dug into the carpet as their hips slammed together.

Harder.

Faster.

Wilder.

Dru gasped, unable to suck in enough breath to fill her lungs. Her hands clenched her hair as she strained, needing something, anything to push her over the edge.

Alex let out a low, guttural groan and thrust harder. Her body rejoiced. He thrust again. All semblance of control was shot to hell. She pressed tight against him, taking him in as deep as she could and swirled. The pressure of his body against her clit, of his dick as deep as it would go, shoved her screaming over the edge.

The last thing she heard as she flew over was his shout of ecstasy.

DRU WOKE SLOWLY, her mind heavy with sleep. She felt as if she was wrapped in a delicious fog, the kind that weighed her body down and filled her with shivery pleasure.

Reluctant to lose this wonderful feeling, but unable to ignore her brain's command to wake, she slowly opened her eyes. She blinked twice, taking in the unfamiliar room, the moonlight slanting across the hardwood floors to highlight a scattering of clothes. The floral silk of her dress tangled with a pair of black slacks on the floor, and a man's shirt dropped not far off. Scraps of lace that'd once been panties announced like a neon sign what'd happened.

Proof that the wildest sex she'd ever dreamed of hadn't been a figment of her imagination.

Alex.

It had all been real.

Her brain was now fully awake and assigning labels to the sensations flying through her body. Her lips were swollen, her nipples beaded, still tingly, against the cool sheet. The delicious ache between her legs was proof that the sex had been anything but tame.

And the weight around her waist was Alex's arm. Muscled warmth, curving tight to hold her close against the hard length of his body. The soft, even rhythm of his breath.

Her heart sped up. She wet her lips and tried not to breathe too deep and wake him.

Oh, God. What kind of woman slept with a man she'd barely known twenty-four hours?

The horny kind, Dru answered herself with a shiver. A very horny, and now very satisfied, woman.

A woman who'd finally had great sex. The kind of sex women dream of, whisper about and never, ever regret. The kind she planned to keep on having until she got on that plane home. For once, she was going to have fun. No meeting of the minds. Screw all that common-ground stuff. This was all about physical pleasure, and the more of it, the better.

Alex's arm tightened around her waist.

Mmm. A tiny part of her that had wished for a moment alone to stretch out on the bed and giggle like a giddy school-girl whose crush had finally noticed her sighed. The rest of her, the part that was warm and cozied up against Alex's very male, very naked and very delicious body, was thrilled he was still there.

Even if she didn't have a single clue what to say to the guy. Except maybe, "More, please."

His hand flattened against her belly, warm and comforting. Like magic, the tension that'd been knotting its way up her spine dissolved at his touch. His breathing changed, warning her just before he nibbled in soft, arousing bites over the back of her neck. Eyes closed as fresh pleasure spun through her system, Dru gave a brief thanks before turning to face him.

He shifted, not letting go but giving her room to tilt her head back and look up into his midnight-dark eyes as she smoothed her own hands across his broad shoulders.

"What do you think? Shall we try to get a little 'bad-der'?" Alex murmured, a wicked smile reflecting the sliver of moonlight in the dark room.

"Badder?"

Could she? Grateful there was no light on her, Dru blushed. She'd tasted nearly every inch of skin on his body. She'd talked dirty, demanded he do her harder and screamed when she came.

How much "badder" could she get?

His hand swept up her spine, making her skin tingle with

need. He curved the other over her breast. Her nipple tightened to a hard, aching peak against his palm.

She'd be crazy to waste a single second of the best sex of her life. After all, flings didn't last forever.

6

DRU WATCHED the seductive play of light dance over Alex's features as he stirred the embers of the bonfire. The crackling heat of the orange flames warmed her, despite the cooling night air and the chill of her still-wet, for more reasons than one, swimsuit. Night surfing, Alex had called it, even though they'd never stood on the board.

Lain, yes.

For almost a week, they'd been all over each other. In each other. Enjoyed each other. And every single time, it'd been over-the-top, mind-blowing.

With one last stoke of the flames, Alex tossed his stick aside and turned to walk toward her. She curled her fingers into her palms to keep from digging them into those broad, sexy muscles and begging.

Begging him for one more orgasm. For one more night. Or worse, for a promise of a month of orgasm-filled nights.

In other words, a future.

"You've got a look in your eyes, like you could light the bonfire with just a glare. Where'd you go?" Alex asked in a teasing tone as he dropped to the blanket next to her.

"Just watching the waves. It feels like magic," she murmured as she gestured to the water, there just on the other side of the dancing fire. "It seems so busy during the day, the sea. But at night, it's softer, filled with possibilities."

Back home, she'd have slapped her hand over her mouth in horror if such a sappy, romantic statement had crossed her lips. But here? With Alex? It felt right. Comfortable. He made her dig deeper, look beneath the surface of their experiences and of herself. And she'd discovered there was a little romance under the veneer she usually showed the world. And since this was her vacation—and her fling—she figured a little romance was a good thing. After all, she'd be packing it up tight and putting it away when she stepped on the plane the day after tomorrow.

She wasn't going to worry about leaving, though.

Not tonight.

Dru sighed again when Alex pulled her close, his chest warming her back as he wrapped one strong arm over her waist to curl her tight to his body.

"It is magic, if you believe. All you have to do is make a wish," he murmured against her skin so she felt his words as much as heard them. Maybe it was that, more than anything, that still made her nervous. She'd spent a week getting naked in almost every position imaginable—at least by her limited imagination—with this man. It was all physical, all day, all night. And yet she could feel his words move through her body, echoing out from her heart all the way to the tips of her toes.

Her stomach twisted tight with nerves she hadn't felt since her first surfing lesson and the implicit agreement to have sex with Alex. Dru sucked in a deep breath of the cool night air and admitted to herself that she had a problem. A big one. She didn't want this to end.

Alex's hand curved tighter around her waist, his breath warming the back of her neck as he nibbled to get her attention.

"What would you wish for, Drucilla?"

Him.

Her heart tripped right over itself at the idea.

Crazy. He wouldn't fit into her real world. Of course, her vacationing, fling-loving self wouldn't fit into her real world, either.

"Success," she finally answered, breaking their ban on discussing real life. It was that or the love stuff. This was obviously the lesser of the two evils. "I want to be the best I can, to do the most I can, and to be rewarded for what I do."

He tensed, just a little, against her back. Oh, God, she should have gone with the painful emotional admission. Dru winced, hoping like mad that he wouldn't try to pick up the real-life-discussion thread.

"Who decides if you're a success, though?" he asked. She didn't know if he'd sensed her tension or if he was just not interested in details. Either way, she was so grateful he didn't ask for details about what she did for a living.

"My peers," she answered, relaxing again. Peers and co-workers at Trifecta, whom she'd known longer than anyone but her mother. People who'd want her to stick around. Who'd value her input. Who'd look at her and see success, not the new girl who never wore the right clothes or said the right thing.

"Ever heard of the perils of peer pressure?" he teased.

"I'm intimately familiar with the concept," she said with a snicker, just a little self-mocking.

"Don't you think you're motivated enough to push yourself to whatever level you want, without kowtowing to the judgment of others?"

Dru started to turn, ready to spill the details of each and every work-related issue and success challenge. Then she caught herself and shook her head. No. No way. Alex thought of her as a sexy beach babe, which was a major thrill. The last thing she wanted to see on that gorgeous face was a squinty stare as he tried to imagine her as a wussy scientist. Or worse, an unsuccessful wussy scientist.

"Self-motivation is good," she said instead. "But unless success is measurable and validated, it's better termed self-satisfaction than success, isn't it?"

She shot him a teasing look over her shoulder as she trailed her fingers down the hard planes of his thigh where it pressed against hers. "There are a lot of things we can do by—and for—ourselves, but isn't it always more fun, and more satisfying, to do it with someone else?"

It wasn't just his grin that let her know he appreciated her double entendre. It was the way he took it as a hint, sliding a finger up the length of her thigh before tracing it along the elastic edge of her bikini bottoms.

Damp heat between her legs, tingling need puckering her nipples. Dru had just had a star-splashed, mind-bending orgasm not more than a half hour before, and here she was, winding right up for another one.

"But if you depend on others as judges, you're subject to their biases, don't you think?" Alex said, his words mellow and calm. As if his stiffening erection wasn't spearing her in the small of the back.

"Listening to others, even with their biases, isn't a bad thing," she replied, so focused on his fingers, she was barely aware of what she was saying. Or that she'd slipped into scientistspeak. "All tests need parameters. Why wouldn't testing one's success be the same? A control that guarantees the results are realistic, are measurable."

"That sounds…safe." He said *safe* in the same tone she imagined he said *boring, blah* and *bland.*

And that was exactly what he'd think of the real her, she surmised with a frown.

"Success without safety is a flash in the pan," she pointed out, her tone snippier than she'd intended. Nothing to rip a gal back from a building climax faster than feeling defensive. "It's a fast thrill, but once it's over, you're stuck having to start again."

Dru forced herself to relax. After all, she wasn't looking to bring Alex into her real world. He was a fling, a boy toy. As long as she kept that in mind, she could enjoy what they had. Fighting back tears, she watched the fire flare, sending sparks harmlessly over the sandy ground.

"I'll stick with secure success," she finally said as calmly as possible. "What about you? What's your ambition?"

"To follow my bliss," he teased.

She rolled her eyes.

"To know I've done my best," he finally said, his words slow and contemplative as he shifted his gaze to the dark waves, "to stay true to myself while making a positive impact in the world. And to have as much fun along the way as I can."

Even though she knew he was only a few years younger than she was, Dru suddenly felt ancient. His words seemed naïve and unrealistic. But his idealism tugged at her heart in a way that worried her.

Still, she'd wanted a sexual adventure. If she had to pay for the adventure with a small piece of her heart, well, she was a big girl. She'd live with it.

Somehow.

Swallowing hard against the unreasonable need for more, Dru watched the black waves wash a gentle dance over the wet sand. Day or night, the waves pulsed.

She told herself to hold tight to that fragile thread of peaceful acceptance. And yet…

"Do you miss it when you leave?" she asked quietly. She didn't have to specify what she meant. As usual, Alex didn't need it spelled out. Instead he lifted his head from his erotic exploration of the side of her throat to look out over the black, moon-drenched sea.

"I'm never away for long," he replied. "And I always come back."

And she wouldn't be coming back at all. As she stared out at the water, Dru admitted to herself that she'd been harboring a tiny hope that maybe they'd meet up here in a few months. Or next summer. Or, well, sometime.

But that'd ruin things. The romance Alex had encouraged her to open herself up to would lose its glow.

No, better to accept that this was it. She wouldn't be coming back.

A part of her wished she could stay longer, then. An insane part, she knew. Even one extra day was an impossible dream. She had responsibilities to get home to. Not only her job, but the mortgage and taxes were due next week on her mom's house and she had to make sure they were paid.

Besides, what made this little sexual fantasy work so well was knowing it was just that. A fantasy. One that had solid parameters and a definitive ending.

Dru blinked fast to clear the unexpected tears from her eyes.

Stupid.

And if she was acting stupid, thinking stupid, it was time to reengage her brain. Dru forced herself to consider the possibilities, what few there were. A quick deduction told her the consequences of even one more day in Alex's company would be too high.

This was it. Their last night. Their last time.

So she'd better make it damn good.

Unwilling to spend any more time wishing for what wasn't when she had the most incredible reality she'd ever experienced, Dru turned quickly to lie back on the blanket. The move unbalanced Alex, who fell across her with a laugh. He caught himself on his elbows and grinned down at her. His smile, just this side of wicked, sent a shaft of desire through Dru's body.

"I want you," she said as she pulled his mouth down to hers. Always a good student, a week of studying his reactions had taught her exactly what he liked. And how he liked it. Her lips melted against his, silky warm and welcoming before she lured his tongue into her mouth. When he gave a low moan, she made a soft sucking action, and at the same time she pressed her hips, covered only in a bikini, against his thigh.

His moan turned guttural.

"Let me deal with the fire and we'll go back to your bungalow," he murmured as he used that magic mouth to drive her crazy. He traced the string of her bikini from her collarbone down to where it met the skimpy triangle of fabric covering her aching breasts. His breath, hot and damp, sent shivers of desire over her flesh.

She wanted him, more now than ever. But she couldn't take him back to her room. If she did, she wouldn't be able to leave.

"No, here," she said adamantly. If she couldn't have more, she'd enjoy the hell out of what she had now. She'd have one more wild fantasy to remember. "Here and now."

His grin fell away and those enticing midnight eyes went even darker. This, she promised herself, was how she was going to remember him. A passionate sex god, looking at her as if she was the answer to every orgasmic dream he'd ever had.

And if that didn't get her through the rest of her secure and successful life, she didn't know what would.

ALEX TRIED to rein in his dick's exultation at the idea and think straight. But he could barely remember his name, let alone pull in the rampant, sharp-edged desire that was driving through him like a runaway freight train.

He stared at Drucilla, appreciating all over again the sharp angles and soft textures of her face. The pure romance of her indigo eyes and pale fairy-princess hair. She was a work of art. A work of very sensual, erotic art.

A work of art who obviously wanted to make a few of his sexier beach fantasies come true.

He was sure she didn't realize what she was asking.

"Drucilla," he murmured as he leaned down to press a soft, teasing kiss over her full lips. "Someone could see us."

"I've wanted to make love with you here, on the beach, since our first kiss," she confessed in a low, husky tone as she trailed one finger over his mouth. Then she arched one brow and traced that same finger down his chin, over his chest to the strained elastic of his bathing trunks.

Alex was pretty sure this was what heaven felt like. Pure fantasy, wrapped in delicious female warmth, with an edge of forbidden sexual need.

Then her finger slipped under the elastic, teasing a soft design over the quivering tip of his erection. And Alex's brain shut off. Fantasies, arguments, even finesse all went flying into the wind. Elbows digging into the sand, he tunneled his fingers through the sea-tangled strands of her hair and lifted her lips to his.

He took her mouth in wild need. Teeth, tongue, lips all melded into one intense, orgasmic crash. He had to have her. He needed to hear her cry out his name, feel her convulse around his body.

After a quick gasp of surprise at the intensity, Drucilla moaned her approval. Sliding her fingers into his swim trunks, she wrapped her long, slender hand over his straining dick. The effect of her night-chilled fingers against his heated flesh sent a zinging flash of need through him. Before he could think twice, he pulled a condom out of the tiny pocket in his swimsuit and let her sheathe him.

He growled in delight at the feel of her cool fingers, but before he could do more, Drucilla wiggled. Alex groaned, opening his eyes to look at her. Her rounded gaze stared back at him, a question in the indigo depths. Before Alex could figure out what she was asking, let alone answer it, she lifted her chin.

"I want on top," she whispered. "I want to ride you like you ride the waves. Power, pleasure and complete control."

He gave her a tight grin as he gripped her hips and flipped her over so fast she gasped out a laugh.

She didn't bother to pull down her bikini bottoms. Instead, she tugged loose the bow on her hip and black fabric fell away. Alex groaned, reaching down to trace the soft curls she'd exposed.

Poised over him, she used both hands to tug the elastic down and free his throbbing dick, then with a wicked smile as her only warning, impaled herself in one smooth, wet thrust.

It took all Alex's control not to come right then and there. The throbbing heat gathered, pulsed, intensified. He'd only last a few minutes.

Knowing he had to bring her up fast and furious, he slid the triangular panels of fabric off her breasts, swirling an index finger around each straining nipple, then flicking the hard nubs.

She gasped, then rotated her hips in a way that tested his control. He plucked at her nipples, then levered himself up to suck one deep into his mouth, teeth and tongue savoring the delicious treat. Her head fell back, soft strands of silken hair tickling his thigh as she moved up, then down. Up again.

He could feel her muscles quivering, tightening around

him. Needing more, he lay back and wrapped his hands over her hips to set a faster, harder rhythm.

So close.

Something nagged in the back of his head, a faint warning. Alex shifted, digging his heels into the sand and raising his hips. Drucilla gave a satisfying gasp of pleasure, her head falling back so her hair rained like glistening moonlight over his hands.

His body climbing higher with every slide of hers, he skimmed his palms along the smooth, bare flesh of her belly to cup her breasts.

The nagging grew stronger. Alex frowned, his passion-glazed eyes narrowing as he struggled to identify the source.

Laughter. He turned his head and squinted. The other end of the beach, about a mile down, at the water's edge. He could just make out a couple strolling along. The wind carried the faint sound of their merriment over the pounding of the surf.

The bonfire blazed between that couple and the glorious sight of Drucilla poised over his body like a sea goddess. But that didn't mean the gigglers wouldn't get an eyeful if they came closer.

"Drucilla," he whispered urgently, knowing how easily sound carried on the beach. "We're not alone."

She slowed her undulating ride, but didn't stop. With a shuddering breath she shook her head as if to clear passion's fog, then met his eyes. It took a few seconds, glorious seconds since her undulations were now tighter, deeper, as she moved in tiny incremental swirls, before his words sunk in.

He gestured with his chin toward their company. She followed his gaze. He pressed his hands onto the sides of her hips, preparing to help her slide free of the pony ride. But she tightened her thighs, gripping his like a vise.

"I don't care," she whispered back. "They're all the way at the end of the resort. They can't see us."

Maybe not in detail, but it didn't take a rocket scientist to figure out what the silhouette of a woman riding a guy in the firelight meant. Alex didn't care if they didn't know exactly who they were, he didn't want anyone getting off on the idea of Drucilla doing sexy times in public.

Filled with a surge of what Alex vaguely recognized as some latent protective instinct, he did the only thing he could. Never one to refuse a lady, especially one who was doing such delicious things to his body, he scooped his hands under her shoulders and in a quick roll switched their positions.

Now she was under him, her legs wrapped around his hips and those glorious blue eyes laughing as she caught her breath.

Her smile was as exciting as the wet heat of her body as it gripped him. He'd never been as turned on by a woman's laughter, by her sweetness, as he was with Drucilla.

He shifted, sliding his still-throbbing erection almost all the way out, then slowly—oh, God, so slowly—back in.

Her amusement quickly faded, passion clouding her gaze as he moved. Alex reveled in the feel of her wet heat gripping him as he slid in, then out. In, then out. His movements in time with the sea's song, he gradually increased the tempo. Her breath quickened, the movement pressing her breasts tighter to his chest. He could feel the fiery prickle of heat where her nipples, still bared from earlier, stabbed into his skin.

Urging him, enticing him. Testing his control.

Control Alex was determined to hold on to. Not only to keep their pleasure private, but to drive Drucilla crazy. To give her the most incredible experience. One that she'd never forget. Just as he never wanted her to forget him, he realized as he shifted, sinking deeper with every thrust.

He pressed his elbows into the towel, the sand beneath it shifting, settling. Supporting his weight as he angled his body, intensified his thrusts. Gave over to the demanding power of his need.

Her movements edgier, Drucilla's eyes closed, her chin lifting to leave her pale throat bare for his lips. Little cries, low and breathy, escaped. Alex's brain shut off. His body took over. He thrust, deeper, faster, harder. His own breath quickened, a guttural cry lodged in his throat.

Drucilla's fingers dug into his hips, her nails a sharp counterpoint to the brain-fogging power of his building climax. He slammed into her now, finesse, observers, hell, everything except Drucilla herself, forgotten as he pounded his way to heaven.

Her body tightened. He felt her orgasm before he heard her cry of ecstasy, the walls of heaven clenching, grasping, pulling him deeper. Drucilla arched. Alex drove deeper. Her nails scraped the bare flesh of his ass as she tried to milk every ounce of delight from his body.

Growling, Alex exploded. Stars flashed behind his closed eyes.

Mind blown, he collapsed against her, barely cognizant enough to shift his weight so he didn't smash her. He buried his face in the silky curve of her throat, the flowery scent of her hair filling his senses. Sweet magic, he thought as his brain slowly reengaged. She was the sweetest of magic. And she needed him.

Her hands now smoothing soft, soothing circles over the small of his back, his shoulders, he sighed. Oh, yeah, she needed him. For sex, of course. Couldn't get better sex than what they had going on here. But for balance. He remembered her crazy talk about success and security. No way was his fairy princess meant to waste herself, her fabulous sense of adventure, on something as uptight as safe success.

He'd have to show her what life was really all about, he realized.

His heart still jackhammering, Alex sucked in a breath, then let it out in a deep, satisfied sigh.

Oh, yeah, he promised himself. There was no way this was ending when Drucilla left. He'd spend tomorrow charming her into agreeing to continue their relationship back in the States.

Relationship, he repeated to himself, waiting, testing. But nope, no freaked-out urge to pat her on the ass and run. Apparently his nerves, along with his heart and his body, were in it for the long haul.

Crazy, he told himself as his brain still floated somewhere on climax cloud nine. It was crazy to think he could be falling in love with a woman he'd know less than a week.

A part of him wanted to tell her, now. To spit it out, take his chance with her reaction. Alex shifted so he could see Drucilla's face, not sure if he was relieved or frustrated to see her lashes curved over her cheeks, her breathing moving from frantic to placid as she slipped into sleep.

Tomorrow was soon enough, he decided, feeling as if he'd just stepped back from a cliff's edge. He'd romance her, charm her, then wow her with his plans.

She wouldn't be able to resist.

"WHAT THE HELL do you mean, she's checked out?" Alex growled, leaning threateningly across the concierge desk. "Don't bullshit me, Juan. Where's Drucilla?"

"She checked out early this morning, took the first flight out."

That didn't make sense. Maybe there was an emergency. Some problem at home.

"Then tell me how to reach her. Phone number, address,

whatever," he snapped, trying to regroup and revise his plans.

"I can't, Alex."

"Don't give me that hotel-policy crap."

"In this case, it's not the hotel's policy," Juan said, apology shining in his dark eyes. "It's the guest's request. She asked that we keep it private."

"She didn't mean from me," Alex said, laughing despite the nasty feeling curdling in his stomach.

"Actually—" Juan fumbled some papers, staring at the disordered pile instead of meeting Alex's eyes "—she said specifically from you."

Alex glared out the window, the pounding surf a pain-hazed blur.

It wasn't supposed to end like this. He wasn't ready to let her go. To let this go. Alex's teeth clenched against the unfamiliar pain ripping at his gut. He'd thought he and Drucilla might actually have a chance. Oh, not forever. He wasn't stupid. But for the next little while.

He had to force himself not to punch the wall as he stormed out the door.

So much for falling in fucking love.

7

"STAND UP STRAIGHT, Drucilla," Olympia chided her only child. "Your shirt is bagging in the front, you don't want to be flashing cleavage, now, do you? You work in a male-dominated field. You have to work harder to get ahead, to command respect. You don't want them to start thinking you're easy or something, do you?"

God forbid.

Nothing drove home *vacation over* like a nagging mother, Dru realized as she yanked another weed from her mother's backyard.

Dru didn't bother glancing down. Her crewneck tee was completely modest. After all, she was home. She spared a brief moment of regret for her silk halter dress. Now *that'd* shown some cleavage. But the dress, like her vacation, was a thing of the past. The real world and all its confining demands were firmly in place again.

Was it any wonder she'd had to leave the country to score decent sex?

Within two hours of getting off the plane, she'd laundered and stored her sassy, sexy vacation clothes. She'd put away her stash of romance novels and spent her first night home tucked into bed with three science journals and a notebook.

And if that wasn't a mocking reminder of what her life was really like without all the incredible sex she'd left behind, Dru didn't know what was.

God, she missed Alex.

"You don't have to tidy the entire garden today," her mother reproved from where she sat, flushed and perspiring on the concrete back step.

"I don't mind." It was a good distraction from pouting over the loss of that mind-blowing sex and missing Alex. And from freaking out that she missed the man even more than she missed the sex.

"I'm getting tired out just watching you, Drucilla. Please, take a break already."

Still patting mulch around the edges of the large clay-potted rose, Dru glanced over, noting the dark circles under her mother's eyes and the heavy droop of her shoulders. It wasn't today's yard work that'd worn her out. Gardening usually recharged Olympia.

And yet the yard had been a mess when Dru had arrived. Which meant her mother had been working overtime at her waitressing job instead of spending time on the one thing she indulged herself in—puttering with her plants.

Guilt made Dru wince, and she focused on getting the mulch just so. She knew her mother would prefer she live here. She knew it was insane to carry the expense of two houses.

But oh, God, she needed her own space.

"You go ahead and rest. I'm almost finished," she replied in a cheery tone, crouching to scoop the deadheaded roses and lavender into the gardening bucket. "Besides, the cosmic string project I'm heading starts tomorrow. I'll probably be swamped for the next few weeks and won't have much time to stop by."

As usual, at the mention of Dru's job, her mother's face

grew gloomy. Dru ignored it, instead turning back to the happier sight of a pile of weeds and dead flowers.

It was pointless to wish her mom would be happy for her. Or hell, even fake being supportive. Nope, Olympia was all about the negatives. Lawrence Robichoux had passed on three things to his daughter. His eyes. His love of science. And, upon his unfortunate death six years back, the care of the woman he'd spent thirty years disappointing.

"You'd have done better to try to get a job with the government, Drucilla. This private lab can fire you at any time, you know. It's hardly a secure position," Olympia said as she came over to help Dru lift one of the large ceramic pots filled with freshly planted herbs to move it to its new sunny perch. "Remember, just because they gave you this project, it's not a guarantee of success. So don't get above yourself. No grandstanding."

"Because there's such an overabundance of grandstanding when it comes to cosmic strings?" Dru retorted, struggling to keep her tone on the joking side of snide.

"It's always better to keep your feet on the ground," her mother chanted, a familiar refrain.

"I think that corner would be perfect for the hibiscus tree we were talking about," Dru said, needing to change the subject. "I had a message waiting from the nursery, they said it'd be in tomorrow. I can borrow Nikki's pickup and get it for you, if you'd like."

"No, no," her mother said as she scooped up the woody bits of jasmine vine they'd trimmed and shoved them into the bucket. "I'm thinking we're just fine with what we have. I don't know anything about caring for those fancy flowers."

Dru frowned. Her mother had a thumb green enough to grow cactus in the snow. One hardy hibiscus tree was hardly a challenge.

She looked at her mom, ready to argue. Then she saw—

really saw—her face. The tension. The worry. The familiar look of fear.

"What happened?"

Olympia pressed her lips white, then plastered on a bright smile. Dru knew that smile as well as she knew her own face. It was the we're-off-for-a-new-adventure smile. The one that always preceded a middle-of-the-night flight. A new school and new friends.

Dru didn't see the look as often now as she had when she was a child. After all, now that she was financially invested, the chances of her mother having to sneak off in the middle of the night to escape eviction was slim.

Her father hadn't been a bad man. He'd absolutely adored his wife and daughter, and he'd been brilliant. When she was little he'd taught college physics. But then he'd lost that job. After a few years, he'd found a job teaching high school biology. But he'd lost that job, too. Eventually he'd had to resort to instructing the occasional science refresher course at the local adult school. He had been a fabulous teacher.

He'd just had a tiny little gambling problem.

One that'd cost his family everything they had. Over and over again.

"Mom? Is something wrong?"

"Nothing major," her mother dismissed. "The washer broke. There was some floor damage, and, well, since the laundry is upstairs, there was a little ceiling damage, too."

"Mom, I can pay for the repairs. And I'll get the new washing machine."

Her mother's smile was shaky. More an acknowledgment that she'd known Dru would offer than a sign of humor.

"I already bought a washer. Things are going to be tight for a bit, though. I've got enough to pay the mortgage, the bills," she said quietly. "I'll be okay. We always are. But I'm going to be working a lot, so I shouldn't bring in new plants right now."

Dru didn't look at the herbs they'd just potted, knowing those didn't count. They were portable. The hibiscus, planted in the actual ground, wouldn't be.

What it would be, though, was a sign of her mother finally acknowledging she was secure. That her home was hers, forever. That she had faith in Dru, in her daughter's ability to secure a living, to be a success.

"Besides," her mom continued, "those full-grown hibiscus trees are so pricey. You can't be throwing money around, Drucilla. You need to save up. Just in case."

Dru grimaced, as usual wondering if her mom's refusal to let Dru buy this place for her outright was really about control over the garden. Instead, they'd bought it together, with Dru putting enough money down to ensure that her mom would be able to afford the monthly payments.

The tension pinching the corners of Olympia's eyes relaxed and she gave her daughter a quick, rare hug. Then without a word she gathered the yard waste, leaving the tools for Dru to put away.

Once her mother's back was turned, Dru let her smile drop. Her spirits fell right along with it.

Any vestige of regrets over leaving Los Cabos early and cutting all ties with Alex were gone. She'd made the best choice. The smart choice.

The only choice.

She had to focus on career success and give this new project one hundred percent. It wasn't about pride or glory. It was about money. Security. A new freaking floor and ceiling.

With that in mind, Dru pasted another smile on her face and dusted the dirt off her hands. "Well, I guess that's one less hole we have to dig. How about some iced tea and cookies?"

DRUCILLA HURRIED down the hall, pulling on her lab jacket as she ran. Because she'd slept through her alarm, her hair flowed down her back in a quick ponytail instead of its usual tidy bun. Four nights home, and each one she'd tossed and turned, at the mercy of hot, sweaty dreams. Winded, she stopped short of the conference-room door to catch her breath, straighten her jacket and adjust the leather messenger bag she carried in lieu of a briefcase. Then she took a deep breath.

This was it. Her first project meeting as lead. Promising herself she'd ignore the butterflies in her stomach better than she had ignored her racy dreams, she plastered on her most friendly, but authoritative, face and pulled open the door.

The chatter in the room dropped, turned to a hissing whisper, then went silent. She was sure everyone was staring because she was late. First time in five years, and it had to be today.

She wanted to blame her mom's dilemma for her sleepless night. But it hadn't been worry over finances that'd had her moaning in a fitful sleep. Nope, it was missing Alex that was making it so hard for her to squeeze back into the neat little box that was her life.

"Sorry, everyone. Alarm issues this morning," she said with a slight shrug, returning greetings as she slipped into her usual chair at the circular table. The chatter started again. She let out a breath of relief and noted neither Dr. Shelby nor their guest had arrived yet.

"Love the tan," Nikki said as she leaned over to give Dru a one-armed hug of welcome. Dru struggled not to squirm, uncomfortable with any kind of public display at the lab. But this was Nikki, whom she both cared about and knew perfectly well didn't give a flip what anyone thought.

"Tell me all about your vacation," Nikki insisted, scooting her chair closer so they could chat. There were about twelve other people in the room, all clustered together in twos and threes. As they all waited for the lab director, no one paid Dru and Nikki any attention, so Dru wet her lips and leaned closer to her friend.

"It was nice," Dru prevaricated.

"Nice?" Nikki arched one perfect brow and tilted her head toward Dru. "Running late? Hair in a ponytail? Just exactly what happened on that vacation of yours?" she asked with a wicked grin.

Dru couldn't help it. She had to share or she'd burst. And really, it was all Nikki's fault, so she deserved to know.

"I did it," she confessed quietly.

Dru watched question, confusion, then clarity flash across Nikki's face. Then Nikki's eyes went huge and her mouth made an O. Not a shocked O or a judgmental O. More like an impressed O, Dru realized with a little tickle of pride.

Look at her, going all giddy over getting slutty on the beach.

"You got yourself a toy?" Nikki clarified.

"Shh," Dru hissed. Then she leaned close and whispered, "Not that kind of toy. Don't make it sound so…dirty. Like vibrators and handcuffs."

Nikki grinned and shrugged. "Did the toy come with those, too?"

Laughter burst out of her before Dru could stop it. The unexpected sound caught the attention of a few of her coworkers. As soon as she noticed, she toned it down to an embarrassed smile. Geez, she'd better get a grip soon or she'd actually deserve her mother's next lecture.

"I'll tell you everything," she promised. "Later."

"Oh, no, you don't," Nikki protested. "You can't leave me hanging like this. One detail," she wheedled.

Dru debated. Then she smiled and pulled her notebook and pen out of her bag. She flipped to a blank page and wrote "Sex on a surfboard."

She didn't get to truly appreciate Nikki's gasp since Dr. Shelby took that moment to enter the room. The director was dapper in his suit and bow tie, all primped and ready to greet their visiting dignitary.

Dru spared a brief hope that A.A. Maddow was as pleasant as he was brilliant. She'd read over a number of his more recent papers and was awed that someone could have achieved his level of success at such a young age. Four years younger than herself, he'd been offered positions with NASA, as well as every major lab in the country.

Not only would it be an honor to have him on her team, but his name alone had guaranteed them the grant funding necessary to ensure her success and security. No, she corrected herself, the project's success and security. But really, weren't they one and the same?

She'd have to thank the director again for this opportunity. She sent Dr. Shelby a welcoming smile and rose to greet him. Halfway out of her chair, she saw another man enter the room. Her eyes bugged out. Her breath caught painfully in her chest. Greeting—hell, thought—forgotten, Dru dropped back into her chair.

Alex? Her playmate, beach lover, sexy naked wild man, Alex?

What was he doing here? And why was he dressed all uptight and businesslike?

She barely heard the greetings being passed around the table. A buzzing filled her head. Color warmed her cheeks at the images of the two of them, naked on the beach. Naked on a surfboard. Naked against the wall.

Then the color drained, leaving her cheeks icy cold.

Naked. She didn't do naked here. This was a fantasy-free zone. There was no way in hell she wanted her coworkers, her team—her boss, for crying out loud—to know she'd had mind-blowing sex on every available surface with a virtual stranger.

Almost hyperventilating at this point, Dru tried to regain control of herself. She ripped her gaze away from Alex's shocked expression and stared at her hands. She forced herself to see only her pale fingers as they clenched a pencil, instead of flashbacks of his naked ass. She recited star clusters, hoping that by the time she'd worked her way through the Milky Way, she'd be able to think clearly.

But one question kept jumping into her head.

Why was he here?

Had he followed her?

"Dru." Dr. Shelby paused in his rush across the room to welcome Alex, to bend close and say quietly, "This is A. A. Maddow. You be sure to show him a good time while he's with us."

Dru was pretty sure her heart stopped. Black spots danced in front of her eyes and a buzzing filled her ears. A. A. Maddow? He couldn't be.

Holy shit. Her sexy beach fling was the rock star?

It was all she could do not to blurt out that she'd already shown him a damn good time. And had the orgasms to prove it.

Too FREAKING UNREAL. Alex struggled to keep the easy smile on his face and nodded in response to the greetings and comments flying around him even though he didn't hear a single word.

He felt as if he'd been riding a sweet wave, then without warning had had a total wipeout and hit his head. Drucilla? His fairy princess. His eyes did a quick inventory and his heart sighed a little as he assured himself it was really her.

Silvery-blond hair snaking down her back in a sleek tail. Indigo eyes, round and shocked. Knife-edged cheekbones and those gloriously full lips that had sent him to so many kinds of heaven.

What the hell was she doing here?

And—his brain slowly reengaged and a frown creased his brow—what was her damn explanation for blowing him off?

Leaving him lying there naked while she scurried off?

Twisting his heart into a knot, then ditching him without even a goodbye?

Anger starting to burn off the fuzzy shock, Alex's stare turned into a glare. He spared the director a nod of thanks when he realized the man was rattling off Alex's bio for those clueless few who might not have heard of him.

Since he already knew who he was, he went back to not paying attention. What he wanted to know, dammit, was who the hell Drucilla thought *she* was. And what she'd been thinking, walking out on him like that.

He opened his mouth, intending to ask just that. Apparently a week of really excellent sex had taught her to read his face. Her eyes, already wide, went huge with horror and she hissed, then shook her head frantically.

Out of the corner of his eye, Alex noted a cute brunette with lots of curls staring between the two of them in curiosity and speculation.

"A.A., welcome," Glenn Shelby said as he pumped Alex's hand like an oil well. "Trifecta is so pleased you're joining us."

Alex struggled to shift his focus from the deviously sexy blonde to the slight, bald-headed director who'd wooed him in as guest physicist with the promise of free rein of the cosmic string project during his tenure.

"If you'd take a seat here," Glenn said, gesturing to a chair directly across from Drucilla, "I'll introduce you to your team."

Other than a brief glance and nod to the people as their names were mentioned, Alex didn't take his eyes off Drucilla.

He waited like a cat outside a mouse hole, until Glenn worked his way around the table to Drucilla. Then he leaned back in his chair and arched his brow.

"A.A., I'm pleased to introduce you to your coleader, D. A. Robichoux. Dru's one of our top astrophysicists. This theory of cosmic strings' gravitational influence on hydrogen gas in space is her baby, so to speak. She'll be seeing it through after you've helped launch the project."

Fury and delight battled for top position in his gut. Alex could see from Drucilla's expression that this was news to her. And, if the tight look in her eyes was anything to go by, the news was totally unwelcome.

"The two of you will need to work quite closely, of course," the director continued. "But I'm sure you'll get along fabulously together."

Drucilla's indigo eyes flashed a hurt protest, then she blinked and the hurt was gone. In its place was ice. Chilly, distant and dismissive.

You'd think she'd have at least clued in to his inability to walk away from a challenge after that week of hot, wild sex. Alex leaned back in the plastic chair and contemplated exactly how he'd deal with her.

An hour later, everyone had been introduced, and the team had been briefed on the project outline. They had two weeks to secure the final funding to create a mathematical model on cosmic strings in relation to hydrogen gas. The project was fascinating. It would, if it succeeded, be another bright feather in Alex's already crowded cap of glory.

But for the grandson of a renowned physicist who'd worked with none other than Albert Einstein, there could never be too many feathers. At least, not according to Alex's grandfather.

Which meant, despite the pain and anger churning in his stomach over Drucilla's walking out on him, he couldn't as easily abandon this project.

He waited for Glenn to wind up the talk, then stood. As if she'd read his mind, Drucilla tapped the brunette on the arm and the two of them got up and rushed to the far side of the room.

As if that was going to stop him.

It took Alex ten more minutes to get through the chitchat and greetings of the rest of the team—all eager to socialize. Finally, when he saw Glenn talking with Drucilla, he took the opportunity. He timed it perfectly, crossing the room as Glenn said goodbye. Obviously the director's departure was a signal that the group could disperse, because it was only the rush of bodies toward the door that stopped Drucilla from escaping.

"Ladies," Alex said quietly as he cornered her and her friend, offering his most charming smile.

The brunette's dimples flashed in a cautious welcome. "Dr. Maddow, I'm a fan of your work. I'm looking forward to the time you'll be spending with us."

Hanson, Alex recalled with a nod. The head of the quantum physics lab.

Unlike Drucilla, who was an astrophysicist. He was still in shock. His sexy fairy princess was actually D. A. Robichoux, a fellow scientist. You'd figure that kind of info would've come up in conversation at some point between orgasms.

So why the hell hadn't it?

"I appreciate the welcome, Dr. Hanson. And I'd appreciate, too, if you'd give me just a second with Dr. Robichoux." He offered his most charming smile and waited. She hesitated until Drucilla gave a tiny shrug, then with a frown, the brunette nodded and stepped out of the room.

Now it was just him and his princess. And the crowd of onlookers, of course. But if he remembered right, she liked an audience.

"Fancy meeting you here," he taunted her quietly. "I have to wonder if this is why you demanded your contact information be kept private. You wanted it to be your little surprise, right?"

Surprise—hell, she looked shell-shocked. Apparently he was just as much a bombshell to her as she was to him.

She glanced around the room at her lingering coworkers and gave a little shake of her head, subtly warning him to be quiet. He stared, amazed as she wrapped herself in a chilly cloak of control.

"Welcome to Trifecta, Dr. Maddow. I'm looking forward to hearing your ideas on my project," she said in clear, concise tones.

"So that's how you want to play it? Well, then let me welcome you, as well." Alex smiled through clenched teeth, then added, "Perhaps Glenn didn't make it plain, but this is my project and I'm the one in charge."

"I'm the Trifecta project leader," she objected, hurt once again flashing in her eyes.

"And I'm the star," he retorted, using the nickname he knew most people referred to him by.

He'd thought that'd piss her off, break through the wall she'd thrown between them. Instead, her demeanor turned even icier as she shook her head.

"We're a team. Both here at Trifecta and for this project. Which means you can check your rock-star ways at the lab door," she said coolly. "And keep in mind, I'm the project leader. You're here as a sort of headliner to draw funds and lend an air of name recognition to the lab."

"It sounds as if you barely need me at all," he murmured sarcastically. "Unlike before."

"There is no before," she hissed, finally showing a fracture in the ice. "As far as I'm concerned, we just met. A.A."

"My mother would be heartbroken to hear anyone use my initials so acerbically," he returned, wanting to see that fracture widen. Hell, he wanted the whole damn ice floe to shatter so he could see if the woman he'd thought he was falling in love with had survived the cold. "Timing is irrelevant. Before or after, you can't deny the need, Drucilla."

As contrary as she'd been compliant in Los Cabos, rather than cracking or melting, her eyes frosted over. Her shoulders stiffened and she gave him a look that hovered at thirty-two degrees Fahrenheit.

"Are you doing this to get back at me?" she whispered.

"For what? I thought you said there is no before," he snapped.

Those glorious eyes flashed once before she offered him an icy glare, turned and strode away. Hell, even her walk was different here. No more loose swing in her hips, her steps were tight and controlled.

Just like the real her, apparently.

The real Drucilla, versus the woman he'd idiotically built a million emotional—and admittedly, sexual—fantasies about. That Drucilla had been sweet and fun, adventurous and sexy as hell. This Drucilla? Cold, dictatorial and inhibited.

Definitely not his type.

So why the hell did Alex have an overwhelming urge to break through that icy exterior and hear her moans of orgasmic pleasure?

8

HER KNEES WOBBLED, but Dru kept her steps measured even though she wanted to sprint for the exit.

Real. Her sexy vacation fling, her hot and wild playmate experience had invaded her real life. She was so screwed. She should have stuck with sucky sex.

Now she not only knew firsthand what great sex felt like and craved it sleeping and awake. But she was craving it with the rock star of astrophysics, the biggest name in her field and her coworker. Which made him the ultimate temptation on earth—and totally off-limits.

Not that he wanted anything to do with her, she admitted with a shaky breath. His anger at her leaving was coming through loud and clear. How difficult would he make things?

Her pulse stuttered as she thought of all the possible ways for this situation to explode all over her life; she focused on the door and the escape it provided.

"Sneaking off again," Alex murmured, catching up with her just as her hand grasped the lever.

Control. All she had to do was maintain control for the next few minutes, then she could fall apart long enough to figure her way out of this mess.

Her mom's lecture on propriety ringing through her head, she pulled on her coolest persona and slanted him a chilly look.

"How is it sneaking to walk away in front of you and a roomful of people? Or is it that you're used to being the first to leave that's got you all uptight?"

"There's nothing uptight about me," he pointed out, looking stung at her insight. He put his hand over hers on the door, effectively trapping her. Heat sparked between them at the touch, her body going warm and wet. Pavlovian reaction, she told herself. Anything learned could be unlearned. "Or did you mean upright?"

Dru rolled her eyes at the lame joke before she could stop herself.

"Cute."

"Thanks," he said with a grin that transported her back to salty surf and hot sands. Then he leaned closer, his minty breath sending tendrils of loose hair fluttering around her face. "But unless you want your coworkers to know just how upright you make me, we might want to take this somewhere private."

Rock or hard place? Unable to help herself, she dropped her gaze to check his assertion. Yep, he was definitely hard and upright.

"All for you," he murmured, seeing where her eyes had gone.

"Lucky me."

And wasn't she an idiot for letting that excite her. It wasn't as if it would last. He was only turned on by the memory of all that beach sex. If this was the first time they'd met, he wouldn't look at her twice.

"We're starting to attract attention, princess."

She winced at the nickname, but turned to smile and say goodbye to her team.

"Don't call me that," she whispered, tugging her hand free then opening the door.

"It's better than the other names that come to mind. After all, it's not like I had any idea who you really were, is it?"

"Unlike you, I didn't pretend to be something I wasn't," she retorted as they cleared the door.

He started to protest, but she interrupted, "Surfer boy."

Alex clamped his mouth shut.

Her triumphant little smile made him laugh and shake his head.

"I *never* pretended to be anything other than who I am," he told her.

"Of course not. It's an easy jump from a footloose surfer boy who waxes philosophical while waxing his...board to a renowned physicist with a rock-star reputation. I can't understand how I missed the obvious."

"Lab or waves, I'm the same guy," he claimed.

"Right," Dru gibed as she flicked her finger over his sedate blue tie. Silk, she realized after she'd touched it. Figured.

The two guys at the end of the hall stopped their conversation and stared, then one whispered something to the other and gestured their way.

Panic tried to snake its way up Dru's spine. This was exactly what she'd been worried about. Next thing she knew, people would be saying the reason she'd been given the leadership position was that she'd slept with the rock star.

Wouldn't her momma be proud then?

"The same guy?" she countered as she hurried around the corner as if she was being chased by the ghost of good-sex-gone-wrong. Alex kept pace easily at her side. "You? Mr. Wolf Award? What was that little thing you were dissing back on the beach? Success? Wasn't that what you'd deemed not worth stressing about?"

"I'm honored you cared enough to remember my words,"

he said softly as he pressed one hand flat against the small of her back to lead her down the hall. Even though he didn't know exactly where they were going. Wanting so badly to lean into his hand, Dru forced herself to step aside, away from the temptingly welcome warmth of his touch.

"Remember?" she rejoined as soon as she stepped through the door of her office. "That kind of irony jumps up to slap a girl in the face, don't you think?"

Dru realized she'd made a huge tactical mistake as soon as he entered, closing the door behind him. The office, always sizable before, was suddenly much too small. Almost claustrophobic. Or maybe it was Alex and his huge...presence, sucking up all the air in the room.

"Irony?" he asked quietly, his tone unlike any she'd heard from him before. But of course it was, she told herself. Famous rock-star scientists were obviously a lot more contained, a lot less romantic, when they had to wear a shirt and slacks instead of a sexy bathing suit.

She ground her teeth together to keep from screaming. At him, at the situation, at fate. It was all so unfair.

"You lied to me," she growled, trying to keep her voice from shaking. "You let me, no, you made me think you were some laid-back, philosophical surfer boy with no ambition bigger than catching the next sunrise wave."

As if in slow motion, Alex's smirky little smile dropped away. He straightened, those broad shoulders that she'd held through many a sexual ride tense.

"Lied, Drucilla?"

"Dru," she corrected. God, right after having her coworkers and team realizing she'd screwed this guy six ways from Sunday, the last thing she needed was anyone being reminded of her full name. In Los Cabos, it'd seemed romantic. Fairytale sweet, even. Here? It was just embarrassing.

He arched a brow, a sardonic look in those once-dreamy

brown eyes. Dru's spine stiffened even more—if that was possible—as she accepted that while he was the same man she'd spent the week with, Alex Maddow was no use-'em-and-lose-'em fling.

Dammit. How many disappointments was she supposed to suck up in one day?

"Look, *Dru,* I don't stress over success. I do what I do, I'm good at it, and whether it leads to success or not doesn't worry me."

It was all she could do not to scream. Here he was, her quintessential fantasy, threatening her reputation with his very presence. He'd accomplished her ultimate career goals, and now he was rubbing his success in her face by telling her how easy it had been. And if that wasn't enough, the hottest, sexiest man she'd ever met was completely off-limits and out of her reach.

She wished, just for a tiny second, that she were a violent woman. Then she could either toss him against the door and have her way with him, or smack him for awakening all these churned-up, impossible needs.

Apparently her conflicting wishes were clear in her eyes. Alex gave her a narrow-lidded look and leaned back against her office door. The reflection of her name on the glass behind his head reminded her exactly where she was and what really mattered.

Work, the project, success. Proving herself at the lab so she could secure her position and continue taking care of her mom. Of herself. Of her future. She didn't even have to try to douse her anger. It drained on its own.

"Well, that's lovely for you," she said with a dismissive shrug. "I'm sure your success will bring many benefits to our project. Trifecta appreciates your participation."

He stared.

Five seconds. She let her smile grow chillier.

Fifteen seconds. Her cheeks were starting to ache, but she kept the smile intact.

Thirty seconds. She didn't drop her eyes, but she did let the smile go. She had to, it was hurting her cheekbones.

At the one-minute mark, she'd had enough. She arched one brow and leaned her hip on her desk, crossing her arms under her breasts and cocking her head in question.

"If there's nothing else, I've got work to do," she told him. Dru was perfectly aware that she was being a bitch, but she couldn't help it.

She'd get a grip. Eventually. After all, a girl needed a few minutes, a pint of Ben & Jerry's and some privacy when she was hit in the face with something like this.

She wanted her private ice-cream minutes, dammit.

"Participation?" he mused.

It wasn't the smooth, innocuous words that sent a warning up her spine. It was the wickedly dangerous look in his eyes. Time to fast-forward to the ice-cream portion of her day. Shoulders stiff, she straightened from her desk and stepped forward to gesture to the door.

She hesitated, then defrosted for just a second. "Look, obviously this was a shock for both of us." The tight anger at the edges of his eyes loosened a bit. "We have to work together and we're both professionals. We want this project to succeed. So we'll make the best of it. The past is just that, gone, and I'm sure we both want to forget all about it, right?"

She was proud of herself. Her words were reasonable. Her tone just shy of teacher to student. Very sensible and calm.

Before she could wrench away her arm patting herself on the back, though, his expression shifted. Oh, sure, the anger was gone. But he got this predatory look, as if he was calculating the amount of time it'd take to get her out of her lab coat.

"Alex—"

She didn't have a clue what she was going to say. It didn't matter, though. He moved so fast, grabbing her arms and spinning her so she was trapped between the door and the looming length of his hard, muscular body.

"Forget it?" he muttered. His hands slid down her arms to bracket her wrists, right there at her hips, so he was leaning over her. She wasn't a short woman and wasn't used to men... looming. That's why the nerves were knotting together in her stomach, she told herself.

"Alex—"

"Forget how you look naked in the moonlight?" he asked, his words low and warm. Warm enough to heat up those knots in her stomach and make her feel all melty inside. "Forget the taste of you on my tongue? The sound of your cries as passion takes you crashing over the edge?"

Her throat as dry as sand, Dru swallowed and shook her head. "It was lovely but—"

"Lovely?" Alex goggled for a second, then he threw his head back and laughed. Despite her irritation, Dru's lips twitched at the sound. He had such a great laugh—infectious, light and free.

Like him, she realized.

And not like her. She was none of those things, which he'd see for himself now. Why that hurt so much, she couldn't say.

"Fine, lovely, nice, peachy keen," she amended, rolling her eyes. "But it's over."

"Because you say so?"

"That would be reason enough," she retorted, wishing he'd back up a little. It was hard to think straight when the heat of his body was wrapping around her like a teasingly sexy hug. "Other reasons would be that vacation flings end when the vacation ends. Or that this kind of thing is wildly inappropriate given our situation. Or maybe that you lied to me."

"Bullshit," he growled. Apparently her argument was too much for his fragile thread of control, because she saw it snap as she looked into his dark eyes. Saw him make a decision.

Dru barely managed to shake her head in protest before his fingers tunneled into her hair. His mouth sprang the trap. Protests evaporated at the familiar taste of him, his tongue sweeping along hers, demanding she respond.

Her brain shut off. Her last thought was that this why Alex was so dangerous to her. He could make her stop thinking with just the touch of his lips. And without her brains, what was she?

In trouble. That's what.

His fingers smoothed her hair while his other hand swept down her body, moving her lab coat aside, and then trailing back up her waist to cup her breast.

Dru couldn't stop the moan of pleasure as he squeezed a familiar, exciting rhythm. She wished desperately that she was wearing something more feminine. There was nothing sexy, or accessible, about her button-down cotton shirt or boring bra.

But he made her feel sexy anyway. His fingers skimmed along the top of her bra through her shirt, then slid, somehow, beneath the edge of her bra, using the friction of the shirt's fabric to tease the aching, needy tip of her breast.

She pressed closer, her hips swirling in a slow, welcoming dance against the hard evidence of his desire. With a purr of approval, she ran her hands over his narrow hips to cup his butt and pull him tighter, closer.

The kiss exploded. Tongues dueled now. His fingers speared through her hair, wrapping around the back of her head to tilt her mouth to the exact position he desired. His other hand made quick work of the buttons at her chest, shoving that fabric and her practical bra aside so he could rub his fingers over her hardening nipple.

Dru wrapped one leg around his thigh for better pressure, rubbing her throbbing core against him and wishing they could get rid of all the layers of material between them.

She needed to feel him. Needed his hands, his mouth on her body, quenching this building fire. The only thought in her head was *more*. More heat, more intensity, more Alex. The man was pure sexual magic.

Dru heard a pounding from far off. As if her heart was beating so loudly, she could actually hear it echoing off the walls.

She easily ignored it and rode the wave of passion.

It wasn't until she felt the thuds against the back of her head that she realized someone was knocking on her office door.

The door she was currently getting hot, wet and wicked against.

"Stop," she gasped in a husky whisper, pulling away from Alex's questing mouth. She turned her head to the side to avoid him when he tried to recapture her lips.

Holy shit, what was she doing? As if the pounding had flipped a switch, her brain reengaged. Dru unwrapped her leg from Alex's thigh and released his ass to push against his chest, trying to get free.

"Stop," she repeated, trying to stifle the panic. God, was she insane? "We're done with this kind of thing."

"It's not over until the flame's extinguished," he said, his words quiet, his tone threatening her sanity as he finally stepped back to release her.

Dru's chin lifted and she narrowed her eyes. Anger at feeling cornered calming her nerves.

Before she could snap at him, though, the door pushed open to bounce against her butt.

Frustrated and flustered, she hurried over to her desk while trying to tidy her hair. All she could think was how the hell she was supposed to explain what they were doing. And why she was all flushed and unprofessional looking.

Then she saw who was in the doorway and relaxed. Not much, but enough that the air could reach her lungs again.

"Oh." Nikki's gaze zipped from Dru to Alex, one brow arched in speculation. "Sorry if I interrupted. I thought your door was sticking again, Dru."

"It's unstuck now," Dru said as hot color poured over her cheeks. Since Nikki had most likely seen their images against the glass door, her friend probably had a solid idea what'd done the sticking. Quickly slipping her buttons closed, Dru moved around Alex without meeting his or Nikki's eyes.

"Well," Nikki drew out, giving Alex a friendly look. "I guess I don't have to ask if you're finding your way around the labs. I can see Dru's tending to your…comfort?"

"Hardly," Dru muttered under her breath. "Alex was just leaving."

They both stared at her as if she was crazy. Nikki's look clearly said *Yeah, right,* while Alex's was more along the lines of a whole lot of frustrated swearwords. Dru didn't care. She needed to think, she needed her ice cream and she needed her space.

Bottom line, she needed him gone.

Alex started to say something, but then he got a better look at the stubborn expression on her face. He wasn't the rock-star brainiac for nothing, apparently, because after a second, he shrugged and nodded.

"We can finish this tomorrow," he promised.

The hell they could. They'd finished it last week and she wouldn't forget that again. But she let it go, instead moving to push the door open wider so he could leave.

"We have an 8:00 a.m. meeting with Dr. Shelby regarding funding and support. I'll see you there."

"At least I know where to find you," he said, the clipped words letting her know he was going to hold a grudge over her Los Cabos departure choices.

A part of her silently mocked that if she'd known how pointless sneaking off would be, she'd have stayed for one more day of mind-bending sex.

But that was also the part of her that'd wanted to wrap him up and bring him home to keep forever and ever. So she ignored it.

"Oh, and by the way, you can reach me at the Hilton," he informed her with a long look as he stepped into the doorway. "Just in case you want to continue this…discussion."

"I won't."

With a smile that called her a liar, he strode out the door, pulling it shut behind him.

Dru's shoulders sagged in relief.

"Care to tell me what I just walked in on?" Nikki invited with a big smile. The dancing humor in her dark eyes made it clear she already knew, and was both amused and fascinated at the idea of Dru acting so out of character.

"That was an oops," Dru muttered.

"Oops?" Nikki's snort of laughter earned her an angry glare. "Is that the scientific term?"

"Psychiatric term is more like it."

"Crazy?"

"That's a good way to put it." Not knowing what else to do with all the pent-up sexual frustration and nervous energy, Dru started pacing.

"Well…" Nikki drew the word out. "I guess I don't have to ask if my suspicions were right. Obviously Dr. Maddow sidelines as a sexy fling."

"Only by virtue of subterfuge." Dru stormed from one end

of her office to the other, turning to stomp the return five steps in quick succession.

"He lied his way into your bed?"

Her angry steps halted, Dru shoved a hand through her loosened hair and tried to figure out how to answer. She wanted to say he had. She wanted to believe he had. It'd feel so much better to believe that.

But, like Alex, she wasn't a liar.

Dru dropped into her chair and gave an angry jerk of her shoulder.

"We didn't make it to the bed the first time," she muttered.

"Details, please."

Dru had to force down her laugh. Leave it to Nikki to find the fun.

"I don't think so."

"Oh, c'mon. You've always shared all the deets of your lousy sexual experiences. Don't think I've suffered through only to be stonewalled on the good stuff."

"He was better than the gasper," Dru offered.

Nikki rolled her eyes.

"Okay, better than the gasper and the wheezer and the groaner put together."

"Oh, please."

Dru propped her elbows on her desk and dropped her head into her hands, her fingers pressing against her temples in an effort to relieve the pounding stress.

"He was incredible," she admitted. "Every woman's dream fling. Attentive, sexy, charming. He was all the good stuff and now he's all the bad."

"Good stuff, bad stuff? He's not a food group or a weird fashion trend."

"No, he's worse."

Dru looked up to meet Nikki's eyes, finally letting all the fear and devastation she felt show on her face.

"He's the man I had the best sex of my life with. He's the one with whom I let my guard down, let see the real me. And he's the biggest mistake I could have ever made."

Compassion and confusion warred in Nikki's eyes. She leaned back, considering, then finally shook her head. "I don't understand."

"He's here. When he was in Los Cabos, he was perfect. I could be what he wanted. Sexy and free and uninhibited. But here, I have to be, well, me."

"That's not a bad thing, Dru."

But it was. She wasn't fun and easygoing and adventurous here. In San Francisco, she was uptight, worried and ambitious. Hardly qualities to turn a guy on.

Not willing to dig into that particular corner of her psyche, though, Dru just shrugged. "Bottom line, he's the worst thing that could happen here. For me, for the project, for my career."

"I don't get it. Why? You've had sex with brainy guys before. Hell, you've specialized in geek sex for years."

"Never someone I had to work with. I've never broken Trifecta's policy and dated anyone associated with the lab," Dru pointed out. "And the geeks were never like this. Those relationships were just that, relationships. It wasn't as if I jumped into bed with them within hours of saying hello. They were…"

"Safe," Nikki summed up.

Dru jerked her shoulder. "Safe or not, they didn't endanger my peace of mind."

Nikki gave her a long, searching look. The kind that Alex gave, that strip-you-bare-and-see-all-your-secrets look.

"Is that peace more important than your happiness?" she asked.

Hell, yeah. But Dru knew her friend well enough to realize that that kind of response would earn her a cozy little pep talk. So instead, she went with a well-practiced shrug and a side step.

"Right now, my career has priority. And that's going to last longer than this…relationship," she said, figuring that sounded better than sexually induced brain drain.

"You're overthinking this. It's not like he's here long enough to be an issue. A few months, max. See it as a gift, like an extended warranty on a really impressive vibrator."

"A vibrator that's almost five years younger than I am, ten times more successful and—if this gets out—perfectly capable of derailing my reputation."

She wanted this project to launch her career, to prove she had what it took to be a leader. She didn't want the success, or failure, of it to be tied in to her sleeping with Alex. Dru knew all it would take was one whisper, one hint of sexy times between the two of them to start that rumor.

Nikki just rolled her eyes, though, in that way that women who had no worries about their own sexuality and attractiveness did.

"Is it that you're afraid you'll have sex with him again? Or that you'll have sex and discover it really wasn't the best sex of your life?"

Dru recalled the fully dressed, near orgasm against the door. No, that was definitely not a viable hypothesis.

"It's one thing to fake being the sexy-fling type for a week," Dru explained, risking the pep talk for total honesty.

"And I didn't even make it the whole seven days," she admitted, throwing her hands up in frustration. "But it's another thing to watch the guy who laid you down on the banks of sexual nirvana and made you scream in delight realize that you're a fake. I'm not the fun, sexy woman he fooled around with, Nik. As soon as he gets to know me, the real me, he's going to lose interest."

"He looked pretty interested to me," Nikki pointed out, shaking her head at Dru's logic. "I mean, it wasn't like the sight of you in a lab coat was doing anything to douse his libido."

"Phantom sexual urges," Dru dismissed.

Nikki gave her a baffled look.

"You know, when someone loses a limb, they sometimes have phantom pains, like a part of their brain imagines the limb is still there. Itching. But it's not real. That's what he was doing. Trying to scratch an itch that wasn't really there."

"Girlfriend, the hard-on that guy was sporting when he hobbled out of here looked one hundred percent real from where I was standing."

It'd felt one hundred percent real pressing against the wet, aching heat between Dru's legs, too.

Argh. She tugged at her hair, trying to make her head work right. He wasn't even here and he was affecting her brain. Because even though she knew there were a million reasons he was horrible for her, she couldn't remember one that mattered.

Thinking time, ice cream and some space. She was sure with those three things, she'd be back in control. She had to be. Because now there was more on the line than just her heart.

Now, her career was at risk. And to Dru, that was much more important.

9

A GOOD NIGHT'S SLEEP, a relaxing breakfast overlooking San Francisco Bay and the mental challenge of an exciting new project were all Alex needed to kick his day off to an excellent start.

Unfortunately, he'd slept like crap, he'd been too irritated to enjoy his breakfast or the view. And the only project he was interested in was cornering Drucilla and settling this mess so they could get back to the incredible sex they were meant to have together.

Unlikely, given that she was still in ice queen mode. Alex leaned back in the chair and stared at the woman across from him, trying to reconcile her with the deliciously sexy beach babe he'd fallen for a couple weeks ago.

He and Drucilla were meeting with Trifecta's director this morning to discuss funding. From the comfortable byplay he'd seen, both when he'd arrived and in the ensuing discussion, Drucilla and Glenn had the same conservative view of where this project was going. A mathematical study on the interplay of cosmic strings, hydrogen gas and gravitational influences. If it could be proven, it'd have a huge impact on all their careers. Trifecta's and Drucilla's, to be sure.

And for Alex, it'd hopefully be the key that would finally

net him his grandfather's seal of approval. The old man set the bar for approval pretty damn high, too. A bar Alex had been trying to reach all his life. A bar he was grateful for, since it pushed him to excel, to take chances. And most of all, to keep moving on, rather than staying in one place and getting stale.

But that approval wasn't going to be offered if Trifecta played this project as a pussyfooting soft sell. The government grants and funding Drucilla had lined up weren't going to cut it. They needed real money.

Instead of saying something, though, Alex bided his time, collecting information and impressions in order to do what he always did. Get his own way.

With this project, he promised himself, and with the sweet and lovely Drucilla.

RATHER THAN THE BOARDROOM they'd shocked each other in the day before, this morning they'd met in the director's office. It was clear that Trifecta put their funds into the lab, not, Alex noted as he shifted again in the uncomfortable chair, into furnishings and frills.

Gone was his fairy princess. Seated on the matching plastic chair, Drucilla resembled so many of the scientists he'd worked with over the years. Her hair, so glorious when draped over his hard, nude body, was pulled into a tight knot at the back of her head. Rather than the vivid colors she'd worn in Mexico, she was dressed in head-to-toe tan. Like toast without butter.

His gaze wandered, from her cool, barely made-up eyes to her flat-heeled, boring shoes. What in the hell was she playing at?

"Is this your attempt to keep me at arm's length?" he leaned over to whisper when Glenn got up to refill his coffee.

"Hiding behind a stereotype isn't going to make me forget how you sound when you come."

Well, that took care of the paleness in her cheeks, he noted with a satisfied grin. Instead of cool distance, now her indigo eyes shot sparks of fury.

Before she could let loose the angry response he could see right there on the tip of her tongue, Glenn returned to his seat. He set his cup precisely in its previous spot on his desk, folded his hands together and looked at the two of them with a benevolent smile.

"Well, we've made a good start. I know Dru can handle the paperwork, A.A. Would you care to tour the labs this morning while she focuses on that? We can gather after lunch to discuss which grants we'll accept."

"Why don't we take this discussion a little further first," Alex said with a smile. "I propose we consider alternate sources of funding."

"Why? We already know where we'll get our funding." Drucilla's look made it clear she was wondering if he'd faked all his awards and accolades. Alex was tempted to remind her that he'd never had to fake anything. And with him, neither had she.

"We have a foundation," he said diplomatically. "It's a solid start, and I'm not saying we ditch it. But I think we could bring in secondary funding, use some other resources."

"We don't need more funding," she said through a smile so tight it had to have hurt her molars.

"We need an infrared supertelescope to prove your theory, don't we?"

Her eyes lit up the same way they had when he'd suggested taking her beyond the break zone to surf the real waves. Challenge, excitement, passion.

God, he loved that look.

Then she hid it behind that freaking wall of ice again. Alex had to clench his fist on his knee to keep from pounding the chair in frustration.

"Trifecta doesn't have access to that type of telescope," she dismissed. "And even the most generous government grant wouldn't provide enough funds to purchase one."

"Right. Like I said, we get alternate funding."

"We don't have the time or the resources to pursue the kind of money it'd take to expand the project that much," she said tightly.

"You might not," he acknowledged, giving Glenn a friendly smile. "But I do."

Glenn frowned. Alex realized that the guy might be even more conservative than he'd originally thought. Which meant he wouldn't get the director's help in double-teaming Drucilla.

"We'll be fine with the original scope of this project." Glenn's comment cemented Alex's observation. "A mathematical model could offer great success in proving the hypothesis."

"You'd do better, and prove more, with the telescope," he told the director before turning his attention back to Drucilla. "With that kind of funding, you could keep the project going for at least a year instead of your proposed three months, too."

For one sweet second her eyes glowed again. It was clear how much the idea appealed to her. Alex smiled, knowing that with her on his side now, any objections Glenn offered would be easily toppled.

Then she shook her head. His jaw almost dropped.

"Three months is enough time to run the calculations, and we can make a solid argument without a telescope," she said.

"For actual, measurable proof to substantiate the theory

and prove your hypothesis, you need a bare minimum of twelve months. And you need that telescope," he snapped.

"We could offer a solid argument through the mathematical model. That would give us a foundation for future projects, as funding was available," she sputtered. "The cost of expanding this to include a telescope is prohibitive, and escalating the experimentation to that level could take years."

"My momma always said nothing worth doing is worth rushing."

"Did your mother also mention the folly of risking that bird in the hand?"

"My mom and I rarely discussed what bushes I put my hands into," Alex deadpanned. It went right over Glenn's head, he noted. But Drucilla, bless her, turned pink all the way to the little string tied in a bow at her throat.

"I'd think one of your major goals for this project would be success," he pointed out, offering his most charming smile. From the look on her face, it made her want to hit him. "You don't get success playing it safe, Drucilla. You succeed by taking chances."

Her gorgeous eyes glared blue flames at him. He was using her own confession to argue against her. And from what he could see, he was winning. It helped that he considered himself an expert on her needs and how to fill them. After all, he'd spent a week getting to know exactly how to read her and how to exploit her needs, in the process making her come over and over and over.

Just the memory of her body, those long pale limbs silky smooth beneath his hands, sent a shaft of desire between his legs, nudging his dick into happy interest.

Bad timing, all around. He had battles to win right now. If he wanted to succeed, both in his funding pitch and later with Drucilla, he'd have to keep that image out of his brain.

"Maybe you see success as taking risks," she replied,

twisting his words just a little. "But I can't believe that short-term accolades are worth more than long-term credibility. If we take on additional funding, we have to offer additional promises. Very public, accountable promises of proving a hypothesis that, to date, has been improvable."

She waited a beat—just long enough for Glenn to let that sink in—then she shook her head. "Why would we risk our reputation when we're already guaranteed the funding to explore this project the way we originally intended?"

Yep, he'd better pull the blood out of his lap. His brain was going to need every drop of it if he was going to win this debate. Besides, he was starting to think he was going to have to accept that this Drucilla, all uptight and bland, was the real woman. The sexy, exciting woman on the beach? Maybe she'd been a product of his lusty imagination.

It was like losing her all over again. Alex shoved the sentiment aside and focused on the one thing he could always count on. His career. He couldn't let her timidity screw it up.

"Because I have connections that could fund the project. People who'd be willing to step in with bigger money. They'd require only the same guarantee required for the government grant."

He could see excitement lurking, right there behind the angry protest in her eyes.

"They're ready to meet with us this week, by the way," he added, laying his trump card on the table with a slow, satisfied smile.

Ten minutes later, he stood to shake Glenn's hand. Drucilla, he noted, kept hers firmly clenched in her lap. He could feel the distance between them widen, and with it, any chance he'd had to convince her that the two of them should pick up where they'd left off. Evidently, Drucilla at work didn't like being cornered as much as Drucilla on the beach.

"I'll need you to attend the meetings as well," he told her, referring to the pitch meetings he'd agreed to set up with some of his wealthier contacts who'd already expressed interest in backing the project.

"Just call my office when they arrive and I'll join you," she agreed.

She obviously intended to make that distance between them even wider. Since he wasn't sure he wanted to close it anymore, he just leaned back in his chair and gave her a smug look.

"Did I say meetings? I should have been more specific. Dinner engagements, probably formal, at restaurants. Like, oh you know, dates," he told her, wondering if the fact that her glare was turning him on made him a deviant of some kind.

"How soon can you set this in motion?" Glenn asked as Alex rose to refill his own coffee cup.

"We can probably have the first one tonight, tomorrow at the latest."

Drucilla stood, her mouth opened and her lower lip trembling. Then she sucked in a deep breath that didn't even ruffle the bow at her throat. "Fine. Just let me know the plans."

With that and a quick nod to the director, she stormed out of the room.

Alex shoved his hands in the front pockets of his jeans and leaned his hip on the edge of the desk, watching her stride away.

Alex was a man well used to arguing, negotiating and cajoling to reach the outcome he wanted, but he realized that while he may have just won on the surface, he'd actually lost.

Drucilla might respect A. A. Maddow's accomplishments and résumé, but she wasn't impressed with them. His brains, his ambition, his focus were all in her way.

So really, he was just a body to her. A sexual toy she'd happily played with during recess for pleasure and entertainment. But now that school was back in session? She wanted nothing to do with him. Serious girls didn't play with toys.

A child prodigy, he'd spent most of his life seeking normalcy. The beach and his friends in Los Cabos had always been his buffer against the demands of his profession, his grandfather's expectations and what he accepted as his obligation to society.

Even so, he'd always been defined by his intelligence. A walking, talking brain.

But Drucilla? A fellow scientist who knew perfectly well the depth and breadth of what that intelligence meant in their field. A woman who, simply by having her name on the same project as him, stood to gain a great deal.

Did she care about him? Obviously not.

She only wanted him for his body.

DRU DIDN'T KNOW what was worse. That Alex had conned her into thinking he was some kind of philosophical, kick-back, go-with-the-flow kind of guy. Or that he'd railroaded control of her project away from her.

That kick-back guy was still invading her dreams and making her want what she couldn't have. And the railroading scientist? He was using her career aspirations to put that very career at risk.

She hadn't seen him since he'd shanghaied the project yesterday morning. Not because she'd managed to avoid him, but quite the opposite—now that she had plenty to say to the renowned A. A. Maddow, he was the one avoiding her.

Drucilla stepped into the posh hotel restaurant and greeted the maître d' with a smile that she hoped didn't look as shaky as she felt. This was insane. Instead of being happily ensconced in her lab or her office, she was here playing beggar in Alex's patron hunt. And not any normal patron hunt, either. She wasn't using her brain, the lab's nice sterile equipment or even pretty color-coded flowcharts for this hunt.

Nope, she was stuck with nothing but her charm.

Shyness shuddered through her like a chill. But she forced herself to stay instead of turning and running.

Normally, she'd have been happy enough to dress up and go out. But not like this. Hell, she didn't even know what *this* was. It was an in-between event where one of her standard beige faculty-event dresses was too lackluster, but one of her colorful vacation dresses would be inappropriate.

So she'd been stuck relying on datewear.

The ubiquitous little black dress.

Her most conservative, the crepe de chine fabric molded comfortably to her slight curves. It was sleeveless and cut in a tantalizing vee at the neck, so she'd paired it with a metallic brocade jacket. The boxy cut took the edge off the neckline and, she hoped, made it modest enough for a business dinner.

She couldn't do anything about the hemline, though. And stubborn pride had made her wear stiletto pumps, even though she knew she'd probably tower over most of her dinner companions.

"Right this way, Ms. Robichoux."

She followed the maître d' through the gentle sounds of upscale dining. Crystal gleamed, carefully arranged greenery provided a semblance of privacy and the even the occasional laugh was muted and refined.

A good place to troll for money, she had to admit.

And there he was, the troll himself, she thought with a little smile as she saw Alex rise from a corner table. She told herself it was hunger that made her stomach tumble to her toes and not the sight of him in his dark suit.

Her step hitched when she realized he was alone at the

table. The clients hadn't arrived yet? As much as she didn't
want to play tonight's game, she wanted alone time with Alex
even less.

But maybe it wasn't a bad thing?

Maybe there was still time to convince him not to risk their
scientific reputations on a flight for the stars and, instead,
settle for some solid down-to-earth kudos.

Then she reached the table and noted the bucket of champagne chilling, the caviar already waiting.

How was she supposed to explain to this gorgeous rock star
that success, to her, meant a steady job, a regular paycheck
and a solid shot at advancing in her career? Not glitter and
accolades.

She couldn't, of course. Not without appearing even stu-
pider than she already did.

"Drucilla, you look lovely," he said. His gaze swept over
her, taking in the loose bun, more a collection of curls than
a controlled style. He studied the conservative jacket and
raised a brow as if to ask if she wanted to remove it so he
could feast his eyes on whatever was beneath. She thanked
the maître d' before slipping into the chair he held out.

Setting her tiny evening bag on the table, she glanced up
to catch Alex admiring her legs. A quick surge of feminine
pride tingled through her.

Unable to resist stoking the embers a little, she slowly,
seductively, tilted one leg to the side to maximize the view.
Then she trailed her fingers from the curve of her knee to
the hem of her dress where it had risen temptingly high on
her thigh.

His eyes went black. She reveled in the dual sense of power
and desire settling low in her belly. She let the maître d' help
push her chair in, so her legs and the view they provided were
hidden beneath the white linen tablecloth.

By the time Alex managed to pull his eyes back to her face, she'd plastered on an unassuming expression.

"Problem?" she asked.

He gave her a long look, a tiny frown of confusion creasing his brow. Then, with a nod of thanks to the maître d', he slid into his own seat next to her.

"You look lovely," he repeated suspiciously. "Why?"

Dru pressed her lips together to keep from laughing, instead raising both brows as if she was shocked.

"Why do I look lovely? What kind of question is that?"

"The kind I feel compelled to ask given that you've gone out of your way to blend in with the wallpaper for the last few days."

Her amusement dissipated in a flash. Wallpaper? Sure, she'd taken a little extra care to distance herself from her colorful beachy persona, the one he'd screwed six ways from Sunday, but that didn't mean she was trying to blend in with the wallpaper.

"Maybe I wanted to impress your potential backers," she suggested tightly.

"No, you didn't," he rejected. He stared through narrowed eyes, then shook his head. "You don't want this deal to go through, so the only impression you'd be trying to make is a bad one."

Dru was actually offended at that. "You think I'd go out of my way to make a bad impression?"

He had the grace to look contrite. "I'm sorry. I was just shocked to see you again."

"You just saw me yesterday," she dismissed, still irked.

"No, I saw Toasted Science Girl yesterday. Tonight I'm seeing you." He stopped abruptly and clamped his lips shut. If he'd been a girl, she figured he'd have slapped his hand over his mouth.

Well, that sure burst the little bubble of anger she'd been nursing so diligently.

Trying to keep a straight face, she had to swallow twice before she could ask, "Toasted?"

"Your beige outfits remind me of unbuttered toast."

The laugh escaped before she could stop it.

His answering smile had just a hint of gratitude in it. As if he'd expected her to jab him in the hand with her fork and wouldn't have even blamed her for doing it.

He reached over and took her hand. Before she could reset her defenses or even start her mental lecture on the million reasons he was off-limits, he gave it a quick, friendly squeeze and released her.

"I'm sorry I put you in this position. I realize this is probably more than you can handle—"

"More than I can handle?" she interrupted, a little confused. Did that have something to do with being beige?

"I checked you out before I agreed to take this project." At her shocked look, he nodded. "I might not have put sexy beach babe Drucilla together with D. M. Robichoux, noted up-and-coming astrophysicist, but that doesn't mean I don't know what you've done. Actually, to tell you the truth, I thought you were a guy. All the people I talked to referred to you as Drew."

Dru stared, her mind racing. She wasn't sure what to think about that confession. She supposed it was easy enough to see how he'd make the mistake. What she didn't see, though, was how it applied to his thinking this evening might be more than she could handle.

She was pretty sure she'd already proved to him just how well she handled everything he had.

Although that probably wasn't what he'd meant.

"That's your excuse for not realizing who I was when

we met in Mexico," she said slowly, trying to establish the point.

"No, that's my reason for not realizing who you were at the beach. And it's my way of reassuring you that even though I know you're a solid scientist, I can understand why you'd be a little worried about being able to handle a project the scope of which I've proposed."

Dru stared.

"You think I can't handle it?"

"I think you're afraid to try."

"I'm not afraid, I'm irritated that you swooped in like a rock star, insisting we change to a bigger stage to accommodate your ego," she retorted.

"Because you don't think you can keep up."

"Bullshit," she snapped, stung.

"Bet?" he suggested silkily.

Bet? This was their career, not a Monday-night football game. It affected their entire lives and he wanted to put money down on it as if it was a horse race?

Was he crazy?

"Terms?" she accepted, unable to resist.

His smile was a slow, wicked curve of his lips. She didn't have to hear the clang of bars slamming shut to realize she'd just been trapped. All she had to do was look at the satisfaction in his eyes.

"You spend the evening being charming and agreeable while I pitch the deal to Buck Blackstone. He's about as nonscience as you can get, but he's rolling in oil money and desperate to get his name on as many projects as he can," he explained. "We act like we're a team and you pretend you're actually on board the supertelescope proposal. Then, if after pretending to love it and listening to me pitching Blackstone, you're not sold on it being the best route for Trifecta, you win."

"I win...what?"

"I'll back off and accept the government grant."

Ooh, wouldn't that be sweet?

But...

"And if you win?"

"You ride with me back to my hotel tonight."

She narrowed her eyes.

"That's it? A ride?"

"That's it," he agreed.

Dru knew there was a catch in there somewhere. She knew the man had a brain the size of Rhode Island and surely had some sneaky strategy all planned out.

Somehow, that only made the challenge more irresistible.

Forty minutes later, Dru was doing her damnedest to win Buck Blackstone over. She'd lost sight of whether she was trying so she could win the bet or simply because the argument had hooked her.

"But think of it," she told the aging cowboy sitting next to her. "The Buck Blackstone Telescope Project," she improvised. "This is going to be the scientific find of the decade and you can be a part of it. Imagine, your name, backing a project of this stature. It would definitely bring even more shoppers to your malls."

Right. She mentally rolled her eyes at that particular line of bullshit. Like any self-respecting teenage shopper would give a rat's ass about a telescope. She noted Alex's smug look.

She notched up the wattage of her smile and leaned closer to Buck.

By dessert, she had him eating out of her hand. And Alex eating her up with his eyes.

"Young lady, I insist you take a ride on my yacht, the *Lady*

Bountiful. Nothing like it in the world. You can even bring your sidekick, here, if you'd like."

Noting the way Alex's mouth tightened, she quickly slid her hand out from beneath Buck's, careful to keep her smile both cool and friendly at the same time.

Who knew her laid-back beach boy could get that rip-a-man's-throat-out jealous look in his eyes?

"What an interesting invitation," she sidestepped. "And you'll have to visit the labs at Trifecta. I'll admit, I'm more comfortable there than I would be on a boat. Seasickness, you know."

Buck gave one of those idiot-man nods, part disappointment, part condescension, part smug satisfaction. Alex's look was all ego. She couldn't really blame him. Considering how many ways they'd done it on the waves, he knew damn well she didn't get seasick.

"Well, I have to say, I wasn't as much interested in the actual project as the write-off when I came into the restaurant tonight," Buck said. "But between the two of you, you've definitely convinced me. What do you think this little project will actually cost in dollars and dinero?"

Alex offered a charming smile and began outlining the financial options while Dru leaned back in her chair and took a cooling sip of champagne.

She couldn't blame Alex for his smug smile. She felt the same. Not because they'd sold the backer on the deal. The guy was as dim as the candlelight in this room, so that hadn't been a hard sell.

But, Dru reluctantly admitted to herself, somewhere between fending off flirtations and volleying the pitch back and forth with Alex, she'd actually started getting excited.

Not about Alex, she lied to herself. About the idea of taking the cosmic string study from a safe, simple process to a more concrete, decisive approach. Doing it her way wouldn't hurt, but it wasn't going to lead anywhere astonishing, either. Not for science, not for Trifecta and definitely not for her career.

And dammit, she wanted excitement.

"Shall we share a cab?" Alex invited a half hour later, his smile wickedly amused.

She gave him a hard look, still trying to figure out when and where he'd outmaneuvered her. One minute she'd been firmly behind government funding. The next she'd been explaining the long-term benefits and myriad options of the telescope as if her life depended on it.

"I drove myself."

"Good," he said, wrapping his hand around her waist as he led her from the restaurant. "You can give me a ride to my hotel."

10

"I'M NOT SLEEPING with you," Dru muttered to him for the third time as Alex followed her out of the restaurant.

He'd love to tell her he wasn't interested just to see that stubborn frown wiped off her face. But he figured the fact that he couldn't keep his eyes off her deliciously long legs would prove him a liar.

"If she won't, I will," an attendant said, giving him a naughty sort of look as if he was imagining Alex naked. It was the first time Alex had ever had that happen, he admitted, unsure if he should be flattered or not. The kid gave him a wink as he took Drucilla's valet stub. "I don't get off until ten, though."

Dru smirked as Alex waved the guy away with an embarrassed grimace.

"I didn't ask you to sleep with me," Alex pointed out. "I asked for a ride to the hotel. The ride you owe me, given that I won the bet."

"You didn't win the bet."

"You sounded pretty convincing back there."

"I agreed to sound convincing," she pointed out in a tone that dropped the temperature about five degrees.

He was starting to understand her better, though. She went

for the chill when she was nervous and trying to stay in control.

"You sounded convincing because you were convinced. You believe the project would be stronger if we switched to a practical model using a supertelescope. Admit it," he urged.

"That was subterfuge."

"Hardly." He rolled his eyes. "I'd know if you were faking it."

She gave him a long, considering look. It was the kind of look no man ever wanted to see. For one brief second, he had actual doubts. Could she have faked it with him? Ever?

His ego shuddered.

"I'd know," he repeated firmly.

She just smiled and leaned back against the flagstone-covered wall next to the valet station.

His head filled with visions of her smiling, just like that, as she was poised over his body. As she leaned in for his kiss. As she rolled away from him with a satisfied sigh. Really satisfied, dammit.

He gave her a narrow-eyed look as he considered the images. His gaze swept from the top of the hair he'd felt draped like silk over his naked hips and down to the lips that'd sucked him like a tasty lollipop. His eyes drifted over the body he'd felt shudder—shudder, dammit—down to the legs that'd held him in a vise grip during those shudders.

No way she'd been faking it, Alex decided. If he knew one thing, it was that people wanted what he had to offer. After all, he'd spent most of his life being used for one thing or another. His brains, his name and, dammit, his prowess.

She was just messing with him. Another brick in that wall she was building to try to keep him away. Or maybe it was revenge for his taking control of the project.

As if he'd let that work. Alex had promised himself

two things when he'd seen Drucilla walk into the restaurant on those glorious legs. That they'd be substantiating the string theory with concrete evidence provided by a supertelescope.

And that he'd feel her long, silky legs wrapped around his waist again.

"Are you giving me that ride?" he asked, challenging her to deny he'd won the bet.

Her jaw worked. Then she heaved a deep sigh that did interesting things to whatever she had going on beneath that glittery jacket and straightened from the wall.

"Fine," she said as the valet pulled up with her reliable blue Volvo. "But if you're looking to get off, you'll have more luck waiting for this guy."

The valet grinned and waggled his brows. Alex gave him a rueful shake of his head as he slid into the passenger seat. He gave the interior a quick glance and grinned. Tidy and well preserved, the ten-year-old car's leather was obviously regularly conditioned, the carpets vacuumed and he was sure the engine was perfectly maintained.

But there, hanging from the rearview mirror, was a dried lily that he knew had once been red, wrapped in a silky ribbon.

Faking it, his ass.

She saw him grinning at the flower and pressed her lips together but didn't say a word. Not that he'd believe her if she'd try to deny that was the same flower he'd given her on their first date. Instead she flicked the ignition on with an irritated slap of her hand, making his smile even bigger. Just yesterday he'd been doubting his judgment and thinking her an ice princess.

"Why physics?" he asked, needing to know what made her tick and figuring that was as good a key as any.

"Why not?"

"A woman like you?" He gave her his most charming smile. "Gorgeous, smart, ambitious? You had plenty of options. Why physics?"

After shooting him a suspicious look, she pulled out of the parking lot. So much for charm. She drove a whole mile before glancing at him again, then shrugging.

"I like science."

"I like surfing," he pointed out, "but it's not a living."

"You know, I thought that myself once," she said with an arch look.

Alex grimaced, not willing to have that particular discussion again. Yes, he'd kept his true career from her. But she'd kept hers from him, too, dammit.

"How about you?"

"Me, what?" he asked.

"Why'd you choose science over riding the waves, since that's something you like so much?"

He was grateful that her words were amused now, instead of angry.

"I never considered anything else," he said with a shrug. "Never had a chance to consider anything else, if truth be told. My grandfather is a physicist. My father was, too, although I don't remember him. It was understood that I'd follow along."

"I thought your mom was…"

He smiled. "A wandering new age fluffy bunny?"

She wrinkled her nose. "Is she really?"

"Mom is…" Alex paused, trying to find the words that would describe the one inconsistent constant in his life.

"Parent issues?" she asked when his pause turned into a hesitation.

"No," Alex shook his head. "I'm just trying to figure out how to explain a woman who uses the pendulum to plan her next road trip and tarot cards to decide what school I should attend."

She shot him a startled glance, then checked again as if gauging his honestly. After taking in his Boy Scout look, she asked, "Were there a lot of schools?"

"You mentioned once that your mom kept her vegetables in flowerpots so she didn't have to leave them behind."

"Yeah?"

"I spent my elementary-school years with my shell collection in a suitcase and comic books in a backpack for exactly the same reason."

"Poor sweetie," she murmured.

Alex realized that he could run with this. The door to her sympathies was cracked open. He could totally play that. He could tell her the story about having to leave the first-place T-ball team midseason. Maybe throw in the one about how they'd moved right after he'd snagged the lead in the Christmas pageant playing the angel on high.

He could trot out all his boyhood disappointments as sympathy-inducing, nooky-guaranteeing ammunition.

Hell, if he threw in the fact that by eight, he'd learned to recognize his mom's "itchy feet" vibe and stock the car with juice boxes and snacks so he'd have something to eat on those inevitable middle-of-the-night adventures, he could turn that nooky into naughty kink.

But...

"It wasn't that bad," he said instead.

The look she shot him clearly said she didn't believe his assertion. He didn't know if it was because he hadn't sold it well enough or if her own childhood of moving around had left her a touch bitter.

"Did you eventually settle into one place? You know, so you could do the normal kid things. Letter in swimming, act in the school play, attend prom with your dream girl?"

"I got to third base with a girl at science camp in Moscow when I was thirteen," he boasted with a grin.

She gave him the same kind of look his mom used when he'd bragged about yet another award. They had just reached the hotel, but instead of pulling up to the front door, she turned right, into the almost deserted parking lot.

Flicking off the ignition, she turned in her seat to face him, the cutest little frown worrying her brow and a sad look of compassion puffing out her bottom lip.

Alex shifted in his own seat, feeling a little naked. His mom had always known he'd hidden behind the boasts, too.

"That had to be such a rough time," she commiserated, patting him lightly on the knee. A little boy inside, one he'd thought he'd left behind decades ago, wanted to climb into her lap for a comforting cuddle.

How freaking manly was that?

Despite his uneasiness, he had to grin. She was so sweet. "I started college when I was fifteen," he reminded her.

"That's my point. Don't you ever feel like you missed out? Or like you have to, oh, I don't know, prove that your willy-nilly nontraditional childhood didn't mess you up?"

Alex hadn't been shipped off to college before he'd had his first shave for being an idiot. She was thinking about her issues, not his.

"Prove to who?" he asked. "I'm doing great. I have a slew of awards, I'm one of the most sought-after physicists in the country and I call my own shots and pick the jobs I take. What's left to prove?"

Or maybe he did have a few issues in there, too. He winced when she shot him a look that said that yes, indeed, she'd caught his version of the he-doth-protest-too-much.

His plan for this ride was to lure her up to his room and get her naked. To feel those amazing legs wrapped around his torso as he drove his way to heaven between her thighs. The noises he'd been hoping for were orgasmic, not sympathetic.

Which meant it was time to change the subject.

"Um, just one question," she asked.

He tensed.

"How, exactly, does one use a pendulum to make decisions?" Her warm smile said that no matter how much he tried to blow it off, she was going to have sympathy for his childhood.

"Swings to the left for yes, to the right for no," he quoted the oft-heard directions. His laugh was tinged with just a hint of desperate gratitude. His gaze met the soft amusement in hers, noting how welcoming she looked with her eyes all gentle and sweet.

Amusement faded. Passion, always simmering just beneath his surface when she was around, heated.

Alex leaned closer and her eyes grew wide. He brushed two fingers down the silky skin of her cheek, then along her jaw to slide beneath her hair. With just those two fingers and his most seductive look, he pulled her toward him.

Their mouths met in a slow, sweet slide of pleasure. He simply absorbed her taste. Time stopped. Space shifted. It was as if they were back on the beach. As Alex's mouth moved in a familiar dance with Dru's, he could almost hear the pounding roar of the waves. Or maybe that was the sound of his own heart hammering away.

As his fingers speared through the curls loosely pinned at the back of her head, he gave in to the need that'd been shoving at him all night. He trailed his other hand—just the tips of his fingers, actually—along the smooth, bare flesh of her thigh.

She gasped.

He shuddered.

Giving her pleasure was the greatest turn-on he'd ever experienced.

Slowly, gently, he pulled his lips from hers and watched as her eyes opened. Hazy with desire, she gave him that I-give-you-permission-to-do-me princess to sex-slave look he loved so much. Unable to resist tasting more, he nibbled his way over the delicate curve of her jaw.

God, he'd missed her. With a small grimace, Alex moved one knee along the seat to try to ease the pressure of his erection against his zipper.

Oh, yeah, he'd missed her like crazy.

"You're delicious," he whispered against her ear, closing his eyes and breathing in the scent of her hair. It reminded him of bonfire smoke and the ocean and midnight walks in a flower garden.

Something inside him, something tucked away deep in his heart, melted a little. He had no idea what it was since he usually made a point to ignore all things heart related.

Drucilla tilted her head to give him better access to that soft, sensitive spot there in the curve of her throat and hummed.

"Let's go up to my room," he invited as he nibbled, ready to explode if he didn't get her naked soon. Or beg, which would be much worse. Because Albert Alexander Maddow had never begged in his life. But for a taste of Drucilla, he was pretty sure he'd actually do it on his knees.

Which would be convenient if the begging paid off, actually.

That visual, him on his knees in front of a very naked, very turned-on Drucilla, sent a surge of passion straight down his belly and into his dick.

"We shouldn't..."

Oh, no. He wasn't letting her protest. He wasn't even letting her out of the car. To hell with the room. He shoved the center console up and in a fast, easy move, pulled her over so she was lying half under him.

Oh, yeah. His dick was so ready to beg.

Alex took her mouth in a hot, wet and wild kiss before she could voice the shocked protest he saw in her eyes. One sweep of his tongue and those eyes fogged with passion and she met his kiss with equal fervor.

Thank God. The ice queen had melted away, leaving behind the sexy fairy princess he'd fallen so hard for.

THERE WERE PLENTY OF intelligent reasons to stop. It was totally insane, argued the protesting voice in her head. But Dru couldn't hear a single one of those reasons over her body's purrs of delight.

God, she'd missed the taste of him. Two days or a million years, she knew she would have lost her mind if she'd had to go another minute without having his rich, sexy flavor on her tongue. Or worse, without feeling Alex's magical hands, those fingers teasing and tempting her to the highest reaches of physical delight.

She shuddered as those fingers moved higher up her thigh, sending shivers of passion coiling tightly between her legs. The kiss deepened. Heat swirled around them, throbbing desire worked its way through her system.

Her brain warned her to stop. They were in a public place, they were colleagues, they weren't the people they'd pretended to be when this kind of thing was okay.

And at the same time, Alex made her want to shove him down, strip him naked and ride him in wild abandon until they both screamed in ecstasy.

As if he could hear her thoughts, Alex flipped the switch. The sweet, almost reverent teasing changed to sexy torment. His palm slid under the hem of her skirt, nails scraping along the crease where her thighs met. Higher, higher, until his index finger traced the lacy edge of her panties.

"I want these," he whispered against her throat. "Take them off."

"You're crazy," she protested. But her breathless words sounded weak, even to her. She cleared her throat and tried again. "We're in the car."

His finger slipped beneath the lace, flicking her wet, swollen bud of desire. Dru's thighs went lax, spreading wider in invitation. But he didn't take it. He pulled his hand back, fingers still tracing erotic patterns against her thighs. But he didn't touch her. Not the way she needed.

"Take them off," he repeated.

She wanted to protest. She wanted to tell him again that he was crazy. But she wanted the pleasure he offered even more. Her eyes locked on his, she lifted her hips in invitation.

"Take them off for me," she instructed.

His eyes locked on hers, he straightened. He released her hair, then glided both hands, palms flat, up the length of her thigh. His fingers pressed, both hands together, at the wet, aching crux of her legs before he swept them sideways to her hips. He hooked a finger under each side and slowly, torturously, slid her panties off her hips, over her thighs and down to her knees.

With a wicked grin, he leaned over to slip the fabric off her calves, pressing his mouth to her bare thigh while he was down there.

A moan escaped before she could stop it. Heart racing, she met his eyes. Nerves and excitement swirled together like dervishes in her belly. Then he leaned forward again, tracing his tongue in the exact spot he'd just kissed.

Dru swallowed, trying to wet her throat. All the moisture in her body had definitely pooled between her legs. Unable to resist, she ran her fingers through the tousled length of his hair where it lay against the back of his neck.

Still holding her gaze, he ran his tongue along the crease where her thighs pressed together. She shivered, her fingers tightening in his hair. He held up her panties like a trophy, then dropped them on his lap before curving his fingers under her skirt and up her hip.

He shifted, sliding up her body, leaving trails of tingling desire, until he reached her chest. He nibbled a sweet path of kisses along the deep vee of her dress at the same time his fingers found their target, swirling around her aching, wet clitoris so fast she gasped.

One finger, then two, slid inside her. He thrust, in then out, twice, then three times while his thumb continued a sweet tormenting rhythm of her swollen bud.

This was insane, she told herself. They needed to stop.

Then he closed his mouth over the sensitized tip of her breast, nuzzling her fullness before he nipped at the peak.

That's all it took. She exploded. The climax ripped through her so fast she couldn't even suck in enough breath to moan. Instead, she gave a keening little gasp, pressing against his hand to hold tight to the sensations rocking through her system.

Oh, God. It was even better than she'd remembered. How was that possible? He was…everything. Too much and not enough, both at the same time.

She needed him more than she needed air.

"We can't do this," she protested when her head stopped spinning. She didn't believe her own words, though. After all, she'd just done it quite nicely, thank you very much.

"We not only can do it," he said, his lips teasing her aching nipple through the thin fabric of her dress and bra. "We do it damn well."

He nipped through the material, sending an edgy shaft of desire spiraling through Dru's already wet and swollen sex.

Damned well, indeed.

Her hips lifted of their own volition, seeking the pleasure only he could provide. More, she realized. She needed more than just his fingers.

Greedy, she chided herself. Her body was still quaking with that delicious orgasm and still, she wanted more. She wanted him inside her. The big, hard, throbbing length of him, pounding a sexual rhythm that would send them both over that fine edge between pleasure and insanity.

"No," she protested, pulling her mouth away from his and trying to catch her breath. "We have to think about tomorrow."

"Let's get upstairs and try out a few of my favorite fantasies," he suggested. "Then we can do it again tomorrow, any position you want."

"That's not what I meant." Exasperation didn't stop her from shivering as his fingers slid down her thigh again. The tingling grew tighter, higher, stronger as his nails scraped gently her swollen, aching sex.

"We work together," she protested desperately, trying to gather her thoughts together long enough to remember the reasons why having another of those sweet orgasms was a bad idea. "We can't… We shouldn't."

Even as she said no, she shifted her head to the side so his lips could reach her throat. The man definitely had talented lips.

"We should," he argued. "We really, really should."

"No."

"Yes."

She shuddered, wanting so badly to give in. But she knew it'd be crazy. The sex, however amazing it would be, wasn't worth the risk of him finding out the truth about her. She wasn't the exciting, uninhibited woman he'd done so well on the beach. And she wouldn't, couldn't, risk what she had here for another round of sex.

Which meant they couldn't do this. No matter how much she wanted to.

"You're a scientist," she pointed out as if she was accusing him of being some kind of degenerate. At the same time, she desperately tugged her skirt back down and tried to adjust the top of her dress so the wet spot wasn't over her sensitive nipple. "You're supposed to be geeky and uptight and have all kinds of sexual issues."

"Geek? Issues?" He stumbled over the words, obviously trying to catch up. Since he was sporting a hard-on the size of a nuclear reactor, she realized the only sexual issue he was probably facing was frustration.

"That's what science guys have," she said with an aggravated push against his chest so he'd let her up. She had to get him off. Off her, she corrected quickly. See, her brain was so stuck on sex she couldn't even think straight. Off. Now. She shoved again. "They have sexual hang-ups and unnatural attachments to Einstein and wheezy, gaspy performance problems."

This time he moved, albeit in slow motion.

Well, apparently she'd found the Off button. Shock had rendered Alex sexless. His eyes did this sort of bugging-out staring thing and his mouth worked but no sound came out. She sneaked another glance at his lap and noted that shock hadn't, however, deflated that lovely hard-on.

She didn't know if she should be proud of finding the button or beat her head against the window a few times as punishment.

Of course, denial of that hard-on should be considered ample punishment enough, shouldn't it? Her mouth watered and her fingers itched just a little, tempting her to take advantage of his shock and screw him senseless.

"Einstein? Wheezy, gaspy? Who the hell have you been dating?"

"Scientists," she said, her tone acerbic. "Wasn't that obvious?"

Shock fading, he shot her a look that made her feel as if he was delving into the secrets of her soul. Feeling naked, she tugged at her skirt again and pressed her knees together.

And was painfully—or pleasurably, depending on whether she listened to her pride or her body—reminded that he still had her panties.

"You know, for a brilliant woman, you have an awfully disdainful view of your own colleagues. What do you do? Handpick losers and geeks for the express purpose of proving that hypothesis valid?"

She opened her mouth to protest, but before she could say a word, he leaned over to press a quick kiss to her lips.

"I'll just have to change your mind," he declared with a wink. Then he released the door latch and told her, "I'll see you tomorrow. Thanks for the ride."

And just like that, he was gone. She watched him stride toward the hotel, his jacket hooked over his shoulder with one finger and his erection apparently not impeding his steps in the least.

It was all she could do not to grab her keys and chase after him. Which, she was sure, had been his diabolical plan. Drive her wild, make her come, then leave her stewing in her own juices—so to speak.

Now Dru did let her head fall back against the driver's-side window.

God, what was she doing? She was certifiable. But even as she desperately grasped for proof that she hadn't lost her mind, her body reveled in the sensation of that climax still shimmering deep in her belly. The muscles of her thighs quivered, and she tried to catch her breath as her clitoris trembled in tiny orgasmic aftershocks.

Sex. Semipublic sex, in her car. She was just asking to get caught. As if it wasn't enough to risk her heart, her hopes. She had to risk her reputation, too.

She swore. Alex was like some kind of sexual addiction she couldn't get over.

11

DRU WHIPPED the pudding so hard, chocolate splatters covered the counter. Three nights ago she'd had a mind-numbing orgasm in the front seat of her car. And what was she doing for wild Saturday-night fun? Making dinner for her mom, who'd gotten sick from an apparent mold issue created by the leaking washing machine. Argh, could this week suck any harder?

Three days. Three long, frustration-filled days.

One minute she'd been wet, panting and having an orgasm in her car. The next, he'd disappeared like a cheap hooker in a vice bust.

Oh, it wasn't as if Dru didn't know exactly what he was up to. He'd gotten her all hot and bothered and left her panting for more. He had her freaking out that he'd tell someone about them. About their relationship, such as it was. Then he'd disappeared without a word. No goodbye, no forwarding information. No response when she'd finally swallowed her pride and called his hotel room yesterday.

It was punishment. He was paying her back for leaving him in Los Cabos. She knew it.

Dru tossed the whisk into her mother's sink, sending another spray of chocolate over the stainless steel.

What a jerk. When she'd left, she'd been ending a vacation fling. And she'd left *after* they'd had mind-blowing all-night-long sex. He might not have been happy with the goodbye, but at least he'd been satisfied.

Dru ripped a brownie into pieces, throwing it into the bottom of a parfait bowl. She tossed spoonfuls of the pudding over the cakey chocolate, growling as she remembered how hard it had been to make that phone call.

She'd spent Wednesday acting like a nervous jack-in-the-box. She'd jumped every time a door had opened, a phone had rung. Sure, Glenn had explained that Alex had been called away. That while they were still waiting on the funding decisions she should have the team get started on the calculations.

But she'd still expected to hear from him. After all, what kind of guy played tag under a colleague's skirt and didn't call her the next day?

Apparently on-call rock-star physicists who had bogus emergencies at NASA.

By Thursday her nerves were long gone and she'd just been pissed. What was he playing at? That, she reminded herself as she shook spoonfuls of Cool Whip over the layer of pudding, was why she'd warned herself to stay away from him.

She'd actually lain awake plotting ways around Trifecta's no-fraternization mandate. Really, she and Alex weren't coworkers since he wasn't employed by the lab. He was a visiting scientist, wasn't he? So she shouldn't have to worry about job security if she had a...fling.

Another fling. She was so addicted to the guy, she was actually standing in her mother's sterile white kitchen—a room the woman refused to paint in case they lost the house—considering ways to have another fling with him. With the man who, for all intents and purposes, held the current success of her career in the palm of his hand. Could you still call it a fling if you'd just had one with the same person?

She licked the chocolate pudding off her knuckle and sighed. That image brought her to her senses. Getting involved with a coworker, even a loosely connected one, was bad enough. Getting involved with a coworker where the balance of power was so unevenly skewed?

All bad. So, so, bad.

She smacked the spoon so hard on the side of the bowl, it almost cracked the glass. Bad. Geeks and wheezers might suck in bed, but at least they were somewhat grateful to actually be there. They had the good manners to say thank-you the next morning, even if in some cases the thanks had been for the scientific breakthrough and not the mediocre sex.

She'd just started shredding the second brownie layer when the doorbell rang. With a frown, she glanced at the clock. Her mother rarely had guests. A neighbor had stopped in an hour ago to drop off a casserole, though. Maybe word was out. If this kept up, she might only get stuck cooking one meal here this week.

Brownie still in hand, she opened the door. And almost squished the chocolate treat when her fist automatically clenched. Alex was leaning against the door frame in a dark blue T-shirt and worn denim jeans that lovingly hugged thighs she'd spent hours dreaming of riding.

"What on earth are you doing here?" she asked when she'd found her voice through the shock.

"Miss me?"

Considering he looked sweeter than the dessert she'd been making, she was forced to privately admit that yes, she'd missed him like crazy.

But a lethal cocktail of anger, humiliation and rejection snuffed out the sentiment more effectively than if it'd been sucked into a black hole.

"How'd you find me here?"

"I bribed someone at County Records."

Her mouth dropped open. "You didn't."

He shrugged, then whipped a bouquet of Peruvian lilies out from behind his back with a grin. "I did. They gave me two addresses, but nobody was home at the other one so I tried here."

Her fingers itched to take the blooms and hold them to her nose and see if they smelled as sweet as they looked. But she could still taste the rejection.

"Why?"

"Because I wanted to see you." He didn't lose his smile, but she could see a hint of impatience in his eyes.

"Really?" She drew out the word to ring every drop of sarcasm from it possible.

"Really," he said, studying her mouth.

She clenched her fingers and chocolate crumbled between the knuckles. She winced and looked at the mess. He followed her eyes, then, smile still in place, lifted the brownie, hand and all, and nibbled at the treat.

She had to work at staying aloof, raising a brow and giving him a questioning look as if her insides weren't melting. After all, how pathetic would it be if she oozed all over him so easily after he'd not only ignored, but practically abandoned, her for three days.

"Mmm," he murmured as he licked the chocolate. "Delicious."

"I bought them from the grocery store," she said in breathless dismissal.

She didn't know what was better, the way he licked her hand, sending wet spirals down deep into her belly. Or the look of frustrated irritation growing stronger in his eyes when she didn't cave to his charms.

Now, wasn't this a nice change after three days of helpless

wanting, of being unable to contact him, of feeling like a horny loser with the sex appeal of a pile of dirty laundry.

"How hard are you going to make this?" he asked, letting go of her hand.

Smart-ass comment or scathing reply? Disinterest or disingenuous? So many directions she could go, so many ways she could salve her ego.

Then she caught the look in his eyes. There was definitely raw passion. But underneath it was a needy sort of hope. Like yes, he wanted to strip her naked and smear that chocolate all over her body so he could nibble it off in tiny wet bites. But that maybe, like her, he was just a little afraid. Afraid of being rejected. Afraid of not measuring up. Or maybe—unless she was projecting, big-time—afraid that he was the only one feeling these fears.

All those emotions that'd seeped through her defenses back in Cabo, the same ones she'd been fighting all week long, washed over her again. Teetering so close to love it hurt, Dru knew she should pull back to regain control.

She looked into the face of the sexiest man she'd ever wished to spend forever with and sighed. He was here, despite the fears she was probably imagining him to have. Was she going to use her own fears, her own feelings of inferiority, as an excuse to chicken out on this relationship?

A possibility that both terrified her and held unspeakable allure. With Alex, Dru knew, she had a chance to explore what a real relationship was. To open her heart, to take emotional chances. And to prove to herself, once and for all, that while she was her father's daughter when it came to science, she was nothing like him when it came to being able to make the right choices and be there for someone else.

She was smart enough to realize she was talking herself into giving this a chance. She was also smart enough to know that not only was it unlikely to go anywhere, but that she'd probably end up hurt one way or another if she gave in to her desire to be with Alex.

What was she going to do? Before she could figure it out, there was a call from above.

"Drucilla?"

Oh, shit.

"Just a minute, Mom," she yelled up the stairs.

"Is there someone here?" And then she heard the only thing that could have made the situation any worse. Her mother's footsteps heading downstairs.

Dru closed her eyes against the amused query on Alex's face and bit her lip. Well, at least now she wouldn't have to worry about how she'd keep from giving in to Alex's overtures. After this, she'd have to chase him down and beg for him to acknowledge her.

Her mom had that kind of personality.

"Who is it?" Olympia asked, holding her robe closed tight as she peered over the banister.

"It's a coworker, Mom. He stopped by with a question."

Alex arched a brow, then tried to look past her. Dru shifted to block his view.

"Is he staying for dinner?"

Horrified, Dru started to yell "No!" But as usual, Alex was quicker. A triumphant sort of glee filled his voice as he said loudly, "I'd love to stay for dinner."

HE KNEW she was irritated, but Alex couldn't help grinning at Drucilla. This was just so perfect.

"What's for eats?" he asked quietly as Drucilla's mother yelled down something about showering before the meal.

"Pig entrails laced with hemlock," Dru deadpanned, still standing in the center of the doorway.

"Yum."

Despite her glare, her lips twitched.

"Drucilla," her mother called again. "Be sure to use the good plates."

Her glare turned into a sigh of defeat.

"You really, *really* don't have to stay," she muttered, finally moving aside. Crossing the threshold, Alex made sure to step close enough that he could breathe in her scent, deliciously layered with rich chocolate.

"Of course I do," he insisted. "I can't disappoint your mother. And besides, the stubborn look on your face gives me the feeling you're going to be hard to pin down again anytime soon."

He loved the way her chin lifted and she gave him a look of frustration.

"Okay, fine. Whatever," she said with a jerky shrug. She eyed the staircase her mother had disappeared up before Alex could see her, then headed toward the back of the house. "It's not like you're going to stick around for long, anyway."

Alex winced. He hadn't thought she'd care if he left for a few days. Despite their encounter in the car, he'd have thought she'd be just as glad to see him gone. The way she'd acted when she'd seen him in the doorway had made him think he was right.

But her eyes told him different. He saw the pain she was trying to hide. That he'd hurt her made him feel about a half an inch tall and a little slimy.

"I had to step in and help an old colleague," he explained, his words rushed and tumbling over themselves. "He called that night, you know, after you dropped me off? He had the swine flu and a huge presentation due Wednesday that related back to a black hole project we'd worked on together."

"You don't have to explain yourself." Her words came out like a statement with a sigh tacked on the end. Alex frowned, not sure if that meant she was impressed, irritated or resigned.

"My hypothesis was key to his breakthrough and subse-
quent funding for this project," he said, as if he was making
an excuse. He wanted to smack himself in the head. He should
have called her. Sure, he might have a Y chromosome, but that
didn't mean he was clueless about how women thought.

Hell, he wasn't stupid.

He was just surprisingly slow when it came to thinking of
anything other than his own needs.

That realization didn't make him feel any less tiny or
slimy.

Nor did the slightly hurt, considering look Drucilla gave
him.

"What?" he asked, his tone more defensive than he'd
intended.

"Nothing. Just wondering if you'll drop everything, or
everyone, to hurry back and help me with some future aspect
of the string project someday."

"Of course," he started to say. Then he sighed and grabbed
her arm before she could leave the foyer. "Drucilla, I'm
sorry."

"For what?"

"For being inconsiderate and hurting your feelings."

"Did I say my feelings were hurt?"

He arched his brow.

Giving him a frustrated look, she finally rolled her eyes
and shrugged, then led him into the kitchen.

Alex didn't know what he'd done that had pushed the
magic button. But whatever it was, he thought as he settled
into a white ladder-back chair to watch her wash the chocolate
off her hands, he was grateful.

For a second, he fixated on the way the water sluiced
over her skin, watching her fingers rub sensually against one
another.

That simple act turned him on. Lecturing himself not to

come across as a sex-crazed jerk, he vowed then and there that tonight, no sex. This visit was all about getting to know Drucilla, not getting to do her.

He finally tore his eyes off her and looked around the house curiously.

"Does your mom live with you?" he asked, eyeing the lush display of potted plants and greenery through the window over her shoulder.

"This is my mom's house," she told him. "I'm not usually here, but she didn't feel well so I came by to make her dinner and stock her freezer."

His heart warmed and he smiled so big, she turned pink.

"Aren't you the good daughter," he teased softly. From her shocked look, that wasn't something she heard too often.

Alex wondered about her relationship with her mother. Close, if she'd drop her Saturday plans so easily. But then he remembered Drucilla's discomfort when she'd mentioned her mother before.

"So you and your mom are tight?" he asked.

She gave him a long, silent look as if she was trying to decipher the answer to that question in his eyes. Then she shrugged.

"I need to finish this," she said, gesturing to the bowls of chocolate and whipped cream and chunks of brownie, clearly wanting to change the subject. "Would you like some coffee while we wait for dinner?"

He eyed the chocolate concoction and remembered the taste of the brownie on her fingers. "Can I have a bite of that instead?"

She glanced at the dessert, then gave him one of those looks. He recognized that look. It was usually preceded by naked moaning and tongues dancing over heated flesh.

He liked that look.

He liked even more when she scooped up a fingerful of the pudding, then dabbed on a bit of whipped cream. He eyed the finger she held out, then the bare skin of her shoulders, highlighted by her sleeveless purple blouse.

She stepped over, stopping between his legs, and lifted her finger. Holding her wrist, Alex brought the finger to his mouth and first licked, then sucked the entire chocolate-covered digit between his lips.

"Delicious," he said.

"Is it?" Her smile was the sweetest thing, a little giddy and nervous, but so sexy.

"You should taste it, too."

She raised a brow, then ran her tongue over her bottom lip. He almost groaned. She lifted her still-chocolate-covered finger and smoothed it over his mouth. This time, he did groan.

She giggled, then planted a hand on either side of him on the table. She leaned over, her blouse gaping. Then her laughing eyes still locked on his, she ran her tongue over the chocolate, sipping it gently before nipping erotically.

He felt that tiny bite as if she'd nipped her way through his jeans. Desire mingled with that delicious sensation of just-this-side-of-pain passion.

To hell with gentlemanly vows and getting to know each other and all that crap. He stood so fast, she almost fell backward. Grabbing her hips, Alex dived into the wild kiss, pouring all his pent-up sexual frustration into that erotic dance between their mouths.

Alex groaned when Drucilla pulled her lips away from his. She sucked in a deep breath that pressed the soft cushion of her breasts against his chest, making him want to groan again.

"We can't do this," she said breathlessly.

"Sure we can."

"No. We can't," she insisted, sounding more like herself as she slid out of his arms. "The shower's off. My mother will be down in a few minutes."

Having to respect that, Alex started reciting the weight of Jupiter's moons to regain control.

"This isn't quite the way I'd hoped to have dinner with you," he confessed with a half laugh.

She bit her lip, then offered a small smile and said, "Maybe tomorrow instead?"

His relief was so huge, it overwhelmed him. Alex's smile damn near split his face and he nodded quickly. A date. They had a date.

Then he heard his own thoughts and shook his head. What the hell was going on? He never got this worked up over a woman. His upbringing had pounded home the fact that all things in life were transient, including relationships.

Especially relationships. Maybe it was his job, that he was never in one place longer than a few months. Or his obsession with science, falling one hundred percent into projects. Probably it was genetic, since no Maddow male had ever had a lasting, healthy relationship. But Alex had learned young that he'd better count on going solo.

Sure, he'd forgotten, temporarily, on the beach with Drucilla when he'd thought he was falling for her. But he'd learned his lesson, hadn't he? This was just about sex. About wanting to taste her a few more times before he moved on.

Which meant he shouldn't be getting excited and hoping for more than just dinner. Alex tried to come to terms with the emotions battering his system.

As if sensing his turmoil, Drucilla eyed him as she spooned chocolaty pudding over a layer of broken brownies.

"Why'd you come by, again?" she asked.

"I thought maybe we could spend the evening together. You know, just hang out."

She made a cute little O with her mouth.

"I was hoping we could get to know each other. The real each other, better," he added when she kept staring.

She tilted her head, started to say something, then stopped.

"The real each other?"

"Yeah. You know, beyond the vacation and work personas."

She narrowed her eyes. "Why?"

He could actually see it. The razor-sharp dive off an emotional cliff, no safe landing in sight. Just a morass of commitment nightmares and painful circumstances.

A dozen blithe excuses fumbled through his mind. Easy outs that would let him step back from the cliff without shame.

"I have feelings for you, Drucilla. I don't know what they are or where they're going. I just know I want a chance to find out," he confessed, despite the voice in his head screaming a warning.

He didn't care about warnings, though. He wanted to go to her, grab her and kiss her senseless. A few kisses and getting rid of that blouse and he was pretty sure he could convince her of anything.

"Let's start with dinner," he finally suggested.

Relief mingled with a giddy sort of happiness that left him feeling a little dorky. Alex grinned. Then Dru did something that made him feel even better. She changed the subject and started talking everyday stuff. He leaned back in the chair, letting the simple joy of just chatting wash away the dorkiness.

Ten minutes later, she'd finished dessert, taken lasagna from the oven and they'd shared first-science-fair stories.

She grimaced when she heard steps overhead.

"Why do you look so unexcited?" he asked with a grin.

"Are you worried about what your mom will think? Maybe you're afraid she'll start planning our future?"

She rolled her eyes. "Hardly. I know she'll hate you. I'm more worried about how you'll feel about me after meeting her."

"Hate me?" His voice rose in shock.

She arched a brow as if to say, *Focus.*

"Feel about you?" he corrected quickly, even though his brain was still stuck on the hating thing. Parents never hated him.

"My mother is...difficult."

"You mentioned that your parents moved a lot." He glanced out the window at the postcard-size lawn and many pots of lush flowers. "And I can see what you meant about your mother's green thumb. How does that translate to difficult?"

She followed his glance as if looking for a description in the yard, then shrugged and faced him again. "Just promise me one thing."

"Anything."

"After dinner, you have to come back to my apartment for hot, wild sex." She leaned over to kiss his slightly gaping mouth. "Promise."

Before he could do more than nod dumbly, she turned to greet her mother. Alex winced a little as he shifted in his chair, using the table to hide his driftwood-size hard-on. Not rising to greet the woman who looked like an older, unhappy version of Drucilla was rude. But greeting her while sporting a predinner woody was probably even ruder.

Five minutes later, he was both presentable and a whole lot clearer on what Drucilla had meant. Her mother was... *grumpy* was the only word that came to mind. It was like having dinner with a little black rain cloud. But a sparkling smile peeked out every once in a while through the gloom.

Beneath the negative attitude, though, it was crystal clear

the woman loved her daughter. Pride lurked behind every critical reminder. Joy sparked when she took Alex through to see the display of science awards.

He couldn't wait to tell Drucilla she'd been wrong. He did like her mom. And he was pretty sure that while *liking* would be pushing the envelope, she at least didn't hate him.

But, damn, he was looking forward to their after-dinner treat anyway.

12

DRU WEAVED HER WAY through the upscale early crowd at the legendary Palace Hotel, unable to stop smiling. Life was good. Since that painfully awkward dinner at her mother's house, and then the awesomely delicious "dessert" at her apartment, she'd spent every one of the last six nights with Alex.

The project was going great, as well. Even Dr. Shelby said so. Her team was moving through the calculations faster than they'd anticipated, which boded well for funding. If they did, in fact, try to push this to the next level the way Alex wanted.

She was having awesome sex regularly. Her mom had actually asked that she bring Alex back for dinner again and had even offered to cook. And, best of all, Dru had woken that morning to a gorgeous, hard-bodied man with his face between her thighs.

Oh, yeah, life was pretty damn good.

She giggled and tucked a loose strand of hair behind her ear, worrying for just a second about leaving it down instead of confining it in a braid.

Alex liked it loose.

Dru reached the romantic gilt-and-crystal entrance of the

Garden Court restaurant, sighing at the curved-glass ceilings and stunning chandeliers before stepping up to the maître d' station. She tugged at her tan linen blazer and quickly dusted her fingers over her taupe slacks.

Alex liked colors on her, too.

Much like their sex life, he didn't always get what he wanted. Her smile, perpetually on the surface these days, flashed again. Sometimes she was the one calling the shots.

Her heels clipped across the marble floor as she made her way past the velvet settees to the linen-covered tables. She stepped onto the thick Oriental carpet, scanning the room carefully. Her gaze finally landed on the elegant brunette she recognized from the portfolio photo. It looked as if Dru wasn't the only one who liked to arrive early.

"Ms. Pownter?"

The potential patron's smile was chilly enough to make Dru want to take notes. Her ice princess act was nothing on this gal's. Dru slid into the chair opposite the woman and smiled, ready to learn a thing or two.

In the next half hour she'd gone beyond impressed to blown away. Charlene Pownter was not only financially savvy, she had more than a basic understanding of the cosmic string project and a firm grasp of the telescope's potential. She was also in total control of the discussion, despite the fact that Dru was the supposed expert at the table.

"I've read your project hypothesis and the suggested means of research. Based on your reputation, and Dr. Maddow's, of course, I think there's a great deal of potential here. I have to ask, do you really believe you need to go to these lengths to prove the cosmic strings' gravitational influence on hydrogen gas in space?"

Dru sipped the orange juice the waiter had just poured, and thanked him before smiling at Charlene.

"I'll be perfectly honest," she said, leaning forward, "to date, we're seeing a great deal of success in producing the mathematical model that should prove the theory quite viable. But as well as that's going, I really do believe we stand to make a huge scientific impact by expanding the project and proving the hypothesis instead of simply substantiating it mathematically."

"And Dr. Maddow?"

Dru didn't figure she was asking about Alex's huge impact.

"What about him?"

"Is he as integral to the project as our telephone conference indicated or was that his ego speaking?"

Dru couldn't stop her snort of laughter. Before she could assure the woman that Alex was a vital component to the project's success, she saw him striding across the restaurant.

"I think you'll be just as impressed with Dr. Maddow in person as you were on the phone," Dru demurred, standing so Alex could find them.

"Ladies, you both look lovely this morning," he said when he reached their table. Dru's lips twitched. Someone had the charm dial turned to High.

Dru settled back in her chair and smiled, ready to enjoy the show.

An hour later, Dru not only had a tummy filled with the best eggs Benedict she'd ever eaten, but she was totally inspired. She didn't know whether it was the delicious food, the elegant atmosphere or the fact that Alex kept slyly rubbing his hand over her thigh, but the more he said, the more on board she was with the project.

"Will you excuse me a moment," Ms. Pownter said when Alex had finished describing the long-term scientific benefits of aligning her name and her organization to Trifecta.

Dru waited until the other woman had cleared the velvet

settees before she let the bubbling giggles free. Grinning, she leaned over and rubbed her hand on Alex's thigh.

"Okay, this is great," she told him. "The more you talk about the project, the more excited I get."

"Excited, hmm?"

She tilted her head to the side, her smile turning naughty.

"Very excited," she murmured, her hand on his thigh changing from enthusiastic to seductive.

"Tell me more."

She bit her lip, glancing around to make sure nobody was nearby. "The sound of your voice when you talk about gravitational pull sends shivers through my body."

He caught her free hand, lifting it to his mouth and pressing a warm, moist kiss to her palm. "Tell me more."

Despite the pleasant tingles his kiss sent over her skin, she pulled her hand away. They'd agreed—well, she'd nagged until he'd given in—that their relationship was to be kept a strict secret.

"The way you spoke, it was pure power. Your confidence, your assurance. Listening to you, I wanted to do anything you asked." She leaned closer, letting her hand slide higher on his thigh. Her fingernails were within stroking distance of his dick, which from the activity beneath his zipper, looked pretty darned intrigued itself. Her gaze locked on his, her eyes soft and sultry as she whispered, "Anything."

"More coffee?"

Dru almost jumped out of her chair, her hand flying off Alex's lap and smacking against the bottom of the table. Eyes watering, she shook her head at the poker-faced waiter, glaring through her tears at Alex's grin.

"I'll have half a cup," Alex said. He waited until the man had moved on before arching a brow. "You were telling me how excited you are?"

Dru took a long and slow breath through her nose, trying

to calm herself. But instead, it just filled her senses with the rich aroma of coffee and made her feel a little shaky, as if she was getting a secondhand caffeine buzz. Nerves, she realized. Whether they were the aftermath of this meeting, or the usual sex-induced hyperawareness she usually had around Alex, she wasn't sure.

"Excited," she said finally when he started to look at her weird. "Yes. I am excited. Thanks to you."

He lifted his fresh cup of steaming coffee, his smile turning cocky.

"I wouldn't have done any of this without your urging," she told him, gesturing to the dish-strewn table and Charlene Pownter's jacket. "You push me, Alex. You make me believe I can do...well, anything."

"You can do anything," he said in that assured, offhand tone that told her he didn't even think twice about it.

"I can," she acknowledged. "I can rock this project. I can woo clients. I can drive you crazy just by telling you how I'm going to use your body after this brunch."

His dark eyes narrowed as his breath hitched a bit. He shook his head as if he was reminding himself where they were.

"Tell me more about your plans," he said softly. Leaning back in the chair, he crossed his arms over his chest, looking very smug.

"Don't let your ego swell," she teased, a little giddy at the idea that she might have some small power over Alex outside of the bed. Or the desk. Or the car. Or, well, anywhere that might lend itself to being a surface for sex.

"I'm energized by the idea of working with the Pownter Institute," she admitted, trying to get them both back on track. "I don't know if it was your compelling presentation or the synchronicity of ideas flowing here at the table. But whatever it was, it hooked me. I'm fully invested now."

Dru saw Charlene returning.

"I want the Pownter backing," Dru said, folding both her hands safely in her own lap, but still leaning toward Alex to make her point. "And I'll do whatever it takes to make it happen."

Amused, she watched his eyes light up with an excitement of his own. After a quick wink, she turned her attention to Charlene.

"Dr. Robichoux, Dr. Maddow, thank you for waiting. I just spoke with my CEO. I'll admit, I'm intrigued by your proposition. But I'm not sure I can justify such a major financial outlay without the guarantee of success."

"Charlene," Alex said with a smile that Dru knew would have melted her own icy walls, but didn't seem to cause a drip in their potential patron's. "You've spent plenty of years dealing with the art and theory of science. You've backed biological research and geological experiments. You've built your institute's reputation on smart choices, yes. But also on well-calculated risks."

"Very true," Charlene said, her voice cold enough to make even Dru shiver. She wished she could keep control with such a chilly panache. "The issue at hand, though, isn't the reputation of my institute. It's the lack of a guarantee that concerns us."

Dru bit her lip, the rich hollandaise suddenly churning in her stomach. Well, this wasn't good. She twisted her fingers together, trying to marshal some kind of convincing argument. But her brain was horribly blank. Her nerves had gotten the better of her.

"Charlene, there are no guarantees in science," Alex pointed out in a reasonable, somewhat amused tone. As if he was verbally rolling his eyes at the woman's caution. Dru wasn't sure if she should thank him or kick him.

"You've seen the prospectus, as well as our hypothesis

and outlines. Our theory is solid. The reputation of Trifecta is unquestionable. The real question here is how confident you feel in the team, wouldn't you say?"

Hazy spots flashed in front of Dru's eyes. She tried to breathe through the sudden tightness in her chest. Her entire career spun behind her eyes in paranoid flashes.

Alex shot her that arch-browed look of challenge. The same look that'd snookered her into surfing. The one that'd tempted her into beachside sex. The exact look that'd sent her dancing around a bonfire, naked. Then later, had convinced her to go along with his putting his damn rock-star twist on her cosmic string project.

Which had brought her to this moment, right here and now in the elegant Garden Court restaurant, sitting opposite one of the wealthiest women in the country, betting the success of her entire career on this pitch.

She hated that freaking irresistible look.

"Ms. Pownter," she started, her mind racing.

"Charlene," Alex said, his charming smile smothering Dru's rescue attempt before she even got started. "We've all been around long enough to have seen a slew of improvable or untenable hypotheses. Oh, sure, they sound great in the beginning. The theory is plausible. The findings are valid. The data and methodology stand up well to scrutiny. But…"

"But?" Dru and Charlene said together.

Alex's smile was pure male satisfaction. The same one he'd worn that time he'd made Dru come three times, then had her begging to go down on him with chocolate sauce.

"But as you know, a scientific endeavor, no matter how sound or intriguing, often makes as much impact in the world as a used tissue. No amount of awards, kudos or acclaim can make it interesting to the general public."

Dru's jaw sagged. Her gaze whipped over to their potential

patron, who was calmly sipping her coffee with a look of placid interest, aka, boredom.

Well this whole deal was obviously going to hell. Dru was pretty sure reaching over and smacking Alex upside the head couldn't hurt things any worse. Curling her itching fingers into her palm to keep her hand in check, she raised her own brow, inclined her head and unable to help herself, asked, "And what exactly does this fascinating assessment of the sciences have to do with our project, Dr. Maddow?"

His grin widened and he gave her a proud look, as if she was a prize pupil who'd just asked the perfect question.

"The achievement we're looking for here isn't just proving the string hypothesis, although that's admittedly an integral key to our success. The bigger goal is, of course, to garner fame, attention and a financial return from a larger segment of society than just fellow scientists."

Dru sighed. Here we go, she thought. The introductory bars to Mr. Rock-Star Scientist's theme song.

"There's actually a specific key to making that happen," Alex said. "That key is all about people. The people on the team, the people promoting the project and the people following its progress. The Pownter Institute understands spin. And there's nothing more spinable than the lady in charge of this project."

Alex and Charlene both turned their heads to stare at Dru. She opened her mouth to ask "huh?" then closed it again, realizing a dense display of cluelessness would probably derail Alex's pitch.

A pitch that had just gotten very interesting. For the next ten minutes, Dru had to use every icy technique she'd ever learned to keep her cool. Alex talked her up. Alex talked her down. He trotted out her degrees, every paper she'd ever published, and waxed poetic on her theoretical skills. By the time he wound up his dissertation on her wonderfulness, Dru was blown away.

Oh, sure, she was impressed with how great he made her sound. And that he knew so much about her. The man had obviously done more homework than just what flavor body oils she preferred.

But what really got her was that he was making this all about her. The woman whose own mother had so many doubts about her ability to succeed that she kept a bedroom ready in case Dru needed to move home.

He'd totally focused on her. It was as if he was pinning the entire success of the project on her abilities. Given that his was a much bigger name than hers was, it was a huge testament to his faith in her.

Dru was pretty sure she actually felt her heart melt. Lips pressed together to keep from grinning like a fool, she stared down at her hands while struggling to regain control.

Had anyone ever said anything so wonderful about her? Understood her so well? And he did understand her. Not just the sexual side of her, although he was definitely scoring top marks there. But the real her.

Dru sighed, dropping her eyes to her half-filled glass of fresh-squeezed orange juice and blinking rapidly. She'd never felt anything like this before. Her entire body was tingly and warm. Her heart was beating so fast, she could feel it all the way to the tips of her hair.

She was either catching the flu, or she had just tumbled over insanity's edge and fallen in love.

ALEX FOLLOWED DRUCILLA into her office, sinking into one of the uncomfortably rickety chairs, and draped his arm over the hard wood back.

He watched her carefully shut the door behind him. Then in the mellowest of ways, she sucked in a deep breath, gave a silent scream and did a funny wiggly dance in place. He grinned at how her arms waved, all out of sync with the tempting swivel of her hips.

Well, someone was certainly happy with the results of their meeting, wasn't she?

"What'd you think?" he asked needlessly, wincing at the tight knots still pinching his shoulders. He wished he knew why he was so tense. He'd rocked the pitch, not only sold Ms. Pownter on the project, but laid the groundwork for her to accept working with Drucilla after he left. Total success, right?

His stiff shoulders argued otherwise.

Luckily, before he could force himself to examine the tension too closely, Drucilla stopped wiggling to smooth her palms over her hips, lift her chin, then cross the room. With pseudo calm, she tucked her purse into a desk drawer then folded her deliciously long body into the chair opposite his.

"I thought it was a good meeting, didn't you?" she said, leaning forward to place her folded hands on her tidy desk blotter and giving him a placid look. Then she giggled and clapped her hands together.

"No, no. It was amazing," she exclaimed, before he could respond. "You should get the science-salesman-of-the-year award. I mean, you know I wasn't totally on board with the expansion. The money, the publicity, the commitment. They add so much pressure, so many additional expectations. And no room for error."

He nodded. After all, she'd been giving him that argument on a daily basis for the last week and a half.

"But now? Now," she said, slapping one of her hands on her desk and sending the blotter spinning sideways, "I'm hooked. I'm so totally committed to this and so totally excited."

And so she was. Energy was practically radiating off her in waves.

"And Charlene Pownter? Man, that woman is an inspiration. She's so together and focused and, well, successful. I had a great time talking with her. Seriously? I want to be her when I grow up. I'd love working with her, learning from her. So what do you think?" she asked, practically bouncing in her chair. "Do you think we have a shot?"

"You were there for a great deal more of it than I was, so you tell me."

He hadn't intended the words to sound like an accusation. But the idea of Drucilla being mentored by Charlene Pownter made his blood run cold. Or maybe it was the image he'd been entertaining for the last two days, of Drucilla, happy and successful when he was gone. Of her exploring her burgeoning confidence with a whole new breed of science guys. Maybe it was the ache in his gut at the idea of leaving her. Or even the lesser ache of knowing he'd soon be giving up a project he found intriguing and challenging.

Whatever it was, it was only adding another layer of knots to his already tense shoulders.

From her big-eyed look, she was just as surprised at his tone as he was.

"She was already seated when I arrived, so we started chatting," she said slowly. "I'm always early, you know that. It was just one of the many ways Charlene and I discovered we're alike."

Charlene. Weren't they all buddy-buddy? Alex didn't like the idea of Drucilla admiring Charlene Pownter quite so much. Yes, the woman was wealthy and determined and successful. Which would be great for the project. But on a personal level, the woman was an ice queen. Totally dedicated to her career, first and last. Exactly the kind of woman Olympia Robichoux would like her daughter to be.

And exactly the kind of woman Drucilla wasn't. Drucilla definitely didn't need chill lessons. She needed fun and encouragement. Support and laughter. To believe in her own talents, but to be willing to take risks and push her own boundaries.

In other words, she needed him. But he wasn't going to be around for long, he reminded himself again.

"Don't get too attached to the idea of working with her," he warned, realizing he'd let his ambition overshadow what was best for Drucilla. He'd been eager to stick a big ole feather in his cap, to impress his grandfather. But not at Drucilla's expense.

"The Pownter Institute requires a longer commitment than Trifecta might be willing to make," he said. "They're going to hold you to higher standards and more rigorous scrutiny than Buck Blackstone would. Charlene Pownter will be more demanding, more exacting than the government grant. She's going to push every one of your buttons."

Her smile fell away. She tilted her head, giving him a searching look, clearly trying to find the reason for his angry undertone.

Alex wanted to tell her to clue him in when she figured it out. All he knew was that there was some kind of fury churning in his gut and a headache the size of a small island pounding in his brain.

"Is something bothering you?" she asked with a direct look that said she wanted an answer, she expected it to be the truth and he'd damn well better spit it out quickly.

He loved that Drucilla the scientist was so strong and straight to the point. Much like Drucilla the hot, sexy fairy princess was in bed.

Which pretty much made her the perfect woman.

Perfect temporary woman, he corrected quickly. Because he was a short-term kind of guy. Between his career, his genetics and his upbringing, he couldn't be anything else.

And that, he realized as he stared into her eyes, noting

the hurt lurking in their indigo depths, was the real issue. He needed to get out of here before he did actual damage.

"I'm sorry, Drucilla." What they had might be short-term, but she was special. Really special. The kind of woman who made a guy think he could actually turn it all around and stick things out.

He winced at the panicky need to run clutching his gut and told himself to chill out. After all, Drucilla knew this was temporary. It wasn't as if she was expecting anything other than the launch of the project and a few really awesome months of intense sex.

"I'm just a little edgy lately," he explained.

Her eyes drifted over his body, as potent as a caress. She ran her tongue along her lower lip, then caught it between those straight white teeth. Alex wanted to climb across the desk and bite that lip himself.

"Edgy? Why?" she asked, her tone husky, her eyes inviting. The look was enough to make him think that maybe, this time, she'd lift her no-kissing-and-definitely-no-sex-in-the-office ban. "I'm sure you're not having any worries about the scope of the proposal. Did you want to analyze the current data? Maybe over dinner? If we bring our notes, it'll look like it's just business and nobody will question us."

And then there was that. Alex clenched his teeth, frustrated that for Drucilla, it always came back to work. He knew he should be more understanding. After all, his career was definitely one of his top priorities. He even understood her reasons for not wanting to give the gossips anything to spread. But did she have to act as if she was embarrassed to be seen with him?

It was enough to make a guy want to claim his woman in a big, public, very gossip-inducing way.

Focus, Maddow. She was right to keep things private.

He *was* leaving soon. No point in sticking her with gossipy backlash on top of everything else.

"I'm just concerned that you might be a little too..." He paused, searching for a way to explain without putting his foot in his mouth. Or anything else. "I'm worried you might be a bit too eager about the Pownter Institute."

"Too eager?"

Her eyes narrowed. Thankfully, the suspicion wiped out that hurt look. She did start tapping her fingers, the rhythm warning him that she was losing her temper.

Alex leaned back in the chair, fighting an unexpected grin. He'd never actually seen the ice princess lose it. Would it be as hot, as sexy, as it was when she lost her cool in bed?

"Let me see if I've got this straight," she clarified in precise tones. "You forced me to step outside my preferred direction for this project, shoving me way beyond my comfort zone. You practically blackmailed me into participating in the patron meetings, nagged me into courting these people who you now claim I'm too eager to work with. Why? Was that pitch a lie? Do you really not believe I'm qualified to handle this project?"

"No," he said, grabbing her flailing hands from across the desk. "Everything I said was true. I believe in you, Drucilla. But like you said, I pushed you. I pressured and twisted this project for my own purposes. That isn't fair to you."

Drucilla wet her lips, nerves dancing in her eyes. She glanced away, took a breath and squared her shoulders, then met his gaze again.

"Alex, I want to do this. I've always taken the easy route. The safe route. Yes, I've aimed for success, but, you know, safe success."

"Drucilla—"

"No, let me finish. I know I argued for the government grant. To keep things easy and pressure free. But you've shown me that some things are worth the risk." She leaned closer, lifting their clasped hands to press a kiss against the back of his knuckles.

"I want to work with the Pownter Institute. I know what's at stake," she insisted, passion making her eyes glow, the same way they did when he touched her. "I want to take the chance. Big risks for big success. I'll make it rock, Alex. For Trifecta. For you. And most of all, for myself."

13

DRU FINISHED PATTING the soil around the base of the hibiscus, then leaned back on her heels to smile at the bright purple blossoms.

Gorgeous.

Nothing said security like roots, right? Even if they were plant roots.

"Drucilla, what on earth do you think you're doing in my yard?"

Dru lost her balance and fell on her ass.

"Mom," she greeted with a grimace as she pushed herself to her knees then brushed the dirt off her butt. "The nursery called again about the special hibiscus order, so I picked it up. I figured I'd surprise you."

From the look of anger scrunching up her mom's face, it was one hell of a surprise. The rip-the-tree-out-of-the-ground-and-spank-Dru-with-the-branches kind of surprise.

"You know how I feel, Drucilla. Is this your way of mocking my concerns?"

Guilt, so easily tapped, bounced right to the surface of Dru's psyche. She had the trowel in hand and was about to dig the plant up before she even realized she'd moved.

"No," she exclaimed. Her words were as much for her own wimpy self as they were for her mother.

It might have been the astonishment of Dru back talking or the fact that she'd back talked at such a high pitch. Either way, her mother's face was a study in shock.

"Please, will you please just believe me, Mom," Dru said, slowly straightening to give herself time to try to figure out what she was going to say. "Nothing is going to happen to the house. You need to stop worrying about it. I've got a steady job, I'm in a solid position with the lab and there's nothing to stress about."

Her mother clamped her arms across her chest and stared.

"Look, I'm heading up a huge project. We're in line to receive backing from one of the biggest institutes in the country. My reputation will be made," Dru claimed, her tone just this side of bragging.

Her mother's glare said just this side was way too far over the line.

"Do you have a guarantee of success on this little project of yours?" Olympia asked bitterly. "Are you so positive that you'll prove your hypothesis?"

Panic tried to worm its way into Dru's gut. But she stood firm and refused. No. Whatever happened, she was going to have faith. In the project's success. In her career potential. And most of all, in herself.

So Dru mirrored her mom's arm-crossed attitude, shifting her weight to the left and setting her chin.

"There are never guarantees in science," Dru said through gritted teeth. "You know that, Mother. Just as you know a failed hypothesis isn't the end of a career."

Her mother looked at her in that way she had that made Dru feel about eight years old. Stomach churning, she lifted her chin higher and tried to stop her lip from trembling.

"Just because Daddy didn't make it doesn't mean I'm a failure, Mother."

"You're your father's daughter. You have the same eyes, the same interests, the same personality. You're practically walking in his footsteps."

Dru's mouth dropped. "That's so unfair."

Olympia lifted her chin, then snatched up a broom and started cleaning the dirty evidence of Dru's recent horticultural venture.

"Life isn't fair, now, is it?"

Dru gave her mother the evil stare of rebellion, perfected in her teen years. It worked just as well now as it had then. As usual, Dru gave up after a few seconds. She puffed out a huge breath of air, then grabbed the dustpan off the potting bench.

"Why can't you support me, Mom?" she asked quietly. "Why can't you believe in me for once?"

The sweeping quickened, her mother's moves getting jerky.

"I believe in this project, Mom. I'm good at what I do and I do have a solid reputation," Dru continued, bending down to hold the dustpan in place. She blinked a few times to clear her vision, then looked up beseechingly. "I've been at the same lab for five years. My papers are well received. I'm heading up a major study before I'm thirty. Why can't you see these things as the positives they are?"

The broom stilled. Dru held her breath.

"You should never count on anything," her mother warned, sounding defeated.

Dru sucked in a shaky, tear-filled breath, then scooped up the dirt, walking slowly to the trash can as if the gloomiest rain cloud was hovering over her head.

"Come have lunch," her mother said, holding open the

creen door. "I just made a fresh batch of your favorite innamon-butter cookies this morning."

Dru wanted to refuse. She wanted to go home, curl up nder her bed and snivel. But as gratifying as that might be, was also pointless. She put the dustpan away, wiped her ands on her jeans and climbed the concrete steps.

As she reached her mom, she frowned. "Fresh this morng? You didn't know I was coming over, though."

"I make some fresh each week," her mother said, heading or the kitchen. "So you always have something to come home ."

And that, Dru realized, was what it was all about. Her 1om wasn't really knocking the possibility of Dru's sucesses. In her own way, her mom was just making sure Dru new she always had somewhere, something, to depend on. Just in case she needed it.

Overwhelmed by emotion, Dru walked over and hugged er mother. Arms wound tight, she rocked from side to side. .fter a brief hesitation, Olympia returned the hug, then :epped back to give her daughter a questioning look.

"That's just a thanks," Dru said. "You know, for the ookies."

RU WAS PRACTICALLY skipping as she made her way down 1e hall to her office. She rounded the corner, her head full of appy thoughts, and almost mowed down her best friend.

"Well, well," Nikki said, laughing as she sidestepped. "Did omeone get lucky last night?"

Dru's eyes widened and she looked quickly up and down 1e hall before hissing at Nikki to quiet down. "I didn't get 1cky," she whispered. "I just had a, well, a really great eveing with my mom."

Nikki's brows shot sky-high.

"Your mom? Olympia Robichoux? She who is never satisfied?"

Dru's lips quirked. With a roll of her eyes, she opened her office door and gestured for Nikki to precede her.

"I went over to do some gardening, then we talked. She was just as discouraging as usual."

Nikki dropped into a chair and stared, giving Dru the when-did-you-go-crazy look.

"I finally realized none of that matters," Dru explained as she sat opposite her friend. It'd taken her half the night to label this giddy feeling, but it was still hard to explain to someone who actually knew how negative her mother was. "My mom has her hang-ups, but they aren't mine anymore. I believe in myself. I've got a solid career I love. I make a good living and have excellent prospects."

Nikki's grin was so big, her dimples almost disappeared. "Hmm, this sounds familiar."

"I know. You've been telling me this for years. But I finally believe it," Dru told her. "I finally believe in myself. And I also believe that the cosmic string project is actually going to make me a star."

"A star?" Nikki looked like a proud momma whose daughter had just scored the lead role in the school play.

"Nik, I'm going to push for the Pownter Institute deal. It's huge," she said as butterflies danced wildly in her stomach. She leaned forward, her hands clasped as she continued. "The bar will be set to the highest rung. The accolades when we actually document the strings' effect on hydrogen gases will be… Oh, man, enormous."

Nikki bit her lip and gave Dru a cautious look. "I love how excited you are. I do. But have you thought this through? You know the percentage of hypotheses that fail. I'm not saying yours will, I'm just saying that maybe you should prepare yourself for all the possibilities. You know the first rule of science. Don't become emotionally invested."

A week ago, that kind of comment would have destroyed her confidence. But now? Everything felt solid. She *was* solid, dammit. Her career star was rising. Her love life was kicking ass. Even her dialogue with her mother was improving.

Which meant even if doubts were biting her in the butt, she could easily ignore them.

"I know the rule," she acknowledged. "But you know what? This is actually one of those win-win deals, isn't it? Having a Pownter backing listed on my résumé is impressive, regardless of the project's outcome. Isn't that worth taking a shot?"

Kind of like what she had going on with Alex. Somehow her career and her relationship with him had become symbolically intertwined. The better she felt about one, the more confident she was with the other. And right now, she was over the moon with both.

"It is worth taking a shot," Nikki confirmed slowly, as if she was seeing the subtext and wasn't sure if she should offer a double warning or just stick with business. "It definitely is. And—" Nikki's face showed her conflicted emotions "—I don't want to discourage your confidence in any way, shape or form."

"But?"

"But what if the project fails?"

Subtext? What if her relationship with Alex failed? Dru's happy mood took on a gray tinge and her stomach turned.

"I'd be fine." She didn't need to see Nikki's face to know she sounded anything but certain. So she squared her shoulders, lifted her chin and stated, "My reputation is solid, my career would stand up. I might not get the accolades or the huge boost, but I'd still have a job. I'd still be secure."

And she'd survive emotionally without Alex, as well. Sure,

it'd be hard to top the incredible sex. And she might not ever connect with another guy on so many levels. But she'd be okay. She wasn't going to start doubting herself again.

"You're sure?" Nikki asked, as if she could read Dru's thoughts. "You'd be okay with that?"

Dru puffed out a breath and forced herself to nod. "I am sure. I have to start believing in myself, Nik. Believing enough to give myself permission to take risks. To have faith that those risks will pay off." She met her friend's dark eyes and nodded. "And yes, to believe that I'm strong enough to handle whatever happens if they fail."

Even as she said the words, she promised herself they'd be true.

ALEX CURLED HIS ARMS around Drucilla's naked waist and sighed deeply. Oh, yeah, this was good. He breathed in the scent of her hair, letting the warmth of it relax him even more than the mind-boggling climax that'd just ripped through his body.

"We need to get moving," Drucilla said, her words a sleepy murmur. "I've got a staff meeting at nine."

"I've got the same meeting." Alex pulled her closer, not ready to let go yet. "We've got time."

"Not if I'm going to shower before I leave." Her words reflected the same reluctance Alex was feeling to get up and start the day.

Probably not for the same reason, though.

He grimaced against her hair and breathed in, needing to hold on to as much of this moment as he could. Not that he didn't think they'd have more sexy times. They would. He was sure they would. After all, their sex life wasn't tied to work. And he'd done what was best.

At least, in his mind, it was best for Drucilla.

He hoped. The sick ball of dread in his stomach warned
m that he was hoping in vain.

So just in case...

"If you need a shower, why don't we see what kind of
ater games we can play to kick off the morning."

A few extra orgasms before she found out his plans couldn't
urt him any, right?

LEX WATCHED DRUCILLA lead the project discussion, pull-
g everyone's input into play, encouraging them to share
eir findings so far, as well as ideas for expanding their
xperimentation.

He'd been pretty well bullshitting his way through the
tch to Charlene last week when he'd raved about Drucilla's
ualifications. Oh, he'd known he was telling the truth. He
st hadn't realized how good she was at doing her job. Not
st the calculations and tests, although watching her run
ose had led to one very memorable, rule-breaking roll on
e lab floor. But now, watching her lead the group, he real-
ed she was simply fabulous.

She encouraged her team, but still kept things on track.
he had the group not only working to their fullest potential,
ut also excited about how far they could push the limits of
sting the hypothesis.

Her smile glowed, filling the room with a bright energy
at made him feel a little gooey inside. Stupid, maybe. But
e just loved how she was totally into what she did.

God, he was getting sappy.

A half hour later, he was still just as sappy, and now way
o turned on for a workday meeting.

"So we're set," Drucilla was saying as she wrapped up
e meeting. As people shuffled out to start their day, Glenn
eld the door open, signaling that Alex and Drucilla wait to
peak with him.

"A.A., good morning," the director said when he reached the conference table. "Dr. Robichoux, how are you today?"

He took Drucilla's vacated seat at the head of the table without a word and set down a folder, clasping his hands over it with a congenial smile.

"I've got wonderful news to share," he said as Dru subtly moved her papers to the left and took that empty chair.

She shot Alex a look, sharing her amusement at Glenn's usual obliviousness. Her expression quickly turned from humor to heat. Alex crossed one leg over the other and grimaced, the horny heading toward that unmanageable-in-company state.

"I thought we'd wind up the project meeting with a little financial powwow," Glenn told them as he handed them each a matching blue folder. "We've solidified our financial decision."

Alex met Drucilla's startled gaze with an infinitesimal wince. He was pretty sure what the director was about to share would eliminate Alex's horny feelings.

Knowing what was coming, he offered Dru his most charming smile, glad to see her blink in surprise, then turn a pretty shade of pink.

Yeah, they'd be fine, he assured himself. He had everything under control. Except the sick feeling in his stomach, but that'd go away just as soon as he knew Drucilla wasn't going to throw that folder at his head.

"The board of directors has met and considered the backing offers," Glenn said, pushing his glasses higher on the bridge of his nose and opening his own folder. "We had a great deal to choose from, which was quite a boon for Trifecta and for which we give complete credit to A.A., his reputation and his wealthy contacts."

Drucilla waggled her brows at him in amused recognition.

"The Pownter Institute offered an impressive package," the director said, folding his hands on the table and smiling. "They not only are willing to buy a brand-new telescope and fund the project for two full years, but they'd welcome new project suggestions by either of you, as well."

Drucilla's eyes went huge and she leaned forward with her mouth open, lips glistening as if she could barely hold back her screams of joy.

"Mr. Blackstone also offered a proposal, in which he'd purchase the abandoned telescope in Mount Shasta to utilize for this project. He'd require, of course, a variety of promotional tie-ins to the telescope in return for donating it to Trifecta."

Drucilla's face went blank except for a hint of disdain clear in the faint wrinkle of her nose.

Well, that wasn't a good sign.

"We've considered both offers carefully," the director continued, his pedantic tone making Alex want to yell at him to hurry up and get this over with. "And taken into account both the good of the lab as well as the strong backing of our guest, Dr. Maddow."

Dru tilted her head and gave him a long, intense stare. Alex almost squirmed, wondering if women came out of the womb knowing that soul-deep, guilt-inspiring look.

"Really?" she asked slowly. "Dr. Maddow had input in the choice? As, what, the visiting short-term guest physicist?"

"Yes. Trifecta is ready to accept the Blackstone offer based on A.A.'s recommendation," Glenn said. "We just need your approval as leader of record."

It was like watching a sci-fi movie where the woman turned to ice. It started in Drucilla's eyes. They went shiver cold. Her demeanor froze, even her skin turned pale.

Alex leaned forward to say something. He had no idea what, but he had to get rid of the chill. But she gave a tiny

shake of her head, clearly not ready for his charming de-
frost plan.

"You know, Glenn, before I sign off with my approval, I
actually have a great deal of input I'd like to offer." Drucilla
shifted her gaze to glance at the director. "But first, I need
to talk to Dr. Maddow. There are a couple of details we need
to clarify."

"Of course, of course," Glenn said as he gathered his folder
and pen. He started to reach for hers, but then patted it and
shot them both a look. "You'll let me know the conclusion,
won't you, Dr. Robichoux?"

She gave a regal nod of her head, then watched fixedly as
the director left the boardroom. Alex waited until the door
shut then said, "Drucilla—"

"Why?" she interrupted. Her quiet tone, so dignified and
at odds with her obvious fury, made him feel like a first-class
asshole.

Her eyes met his again and the fury he saw there made
him wish briefly for her previous icy demeanor.

"Look, I know the Pownter deal would be great. The
money, the prestige, the scientific possibilities," he said, his
words tumbling over each other, he was talking so fast. "But
it also came with intolerable strings."

"Intolerable in what way?" She didn't sound curious,
though. Just…pissed.

"When I spoke with Charlene Pownter yesterday, she informed me that yes, they'd fund the project. But in doing so,
they'd require not just you, but both of us, to serve on it for
the duration."

Sure, sticking around would have given him time to make
certain Charlene Pownter's influence didn't ruin Drucilla.
But that was out of the question. And luckily, that had been
enough for him to refuse the deal.

"And the problem is?" she said, tilting her head to the side.

"The problem is that she's too controlling. Her offer is way over and above what we'd asked for. That's a bad sign," he claimed.

She looked as if she wanted to throw something at his head. But all she did was silently raise a brow. A trickle of sweat slid down his spine. Her control was a little scary.

Finally, he confessed, "The problem is that the duration is two years. The problem is that I don't commit to long-term projects."

Drucilla nodded, as if he'd just confirmed a hypothesis she'd been working on. Then she leaned forward and asked, "So really, the problem is...*you*."

Alex frowned, his need to pacify her starting to grow ragged around the edges.

"Look, this is a win-win deal," he said, not quite willing to give up yet. He put on his most persuasive smile. "Buck's money, my name, the project will be termed a success right there."

"Money and a name won't guarantee results," she pointed out.

"You know how this works, Drucilla. The results could take years. I'm giving you a shot at having all the years you need to get them. Like a success safety net, if you will."

She stared at him. The look in her blue eyes wasn't the chill he'd learned to recognize as a mask for her insecurity. It was razor-sharp ice that sent a shiver through him. Stupid, Alex told himself. He was giving her exactly what she wanted. The safest route to long-term security. She should be thanking him, not giving him the evil eye.

"A safety net? With the choices between taking the bus, aka the grant, buying an unimpressive but probably reliable used car, aka Blackstone, or being offered a luxury sports coupe along with free gas and insurance for two years, you consider the used car the choice?" she asked icily. "And all because, what? It's the most convenient for you? Correct me if I'm wrong, but you seem to be operating under the assumption that this entire project hinges on you and you alone."

He'd actually started to nod before he heard the words play out in his head.

"I didn't make any such assumption," he snapped, offended.

"You didn't voice it," she corrected, crossing her arms over her chest. "But you've been thinking it from the beginning."

"If you're so good at reading minds, why didn't you figure out who I was back on the beach?" he challenged, trying to make it sound teasing. If the hard look in her eye was any indication, though, his attempt flopped.

"Tell me, Alex, what do you see as the overall goal of the cosmic string project?"

Mind racing, he shifted in his seat. He'd served on boards, made presentations to huge crowds and once actually landed a spot on *Jeopardy*. But he'd never felt quite so nervous searching for just the right answer to a particular question.

"The overall goal is to definitively describe a cosmic string's influence on hydrogen gas in space."

She tilted her head to one side. "Did you memorize the entire funding proposal or are you only going to give me a few of the choicer direct quotes?"

That did it. Alex shoved away from the table, his chair skidding back to slam into the wall behind him.

"That's enough," he stated.

"Enough?" she retorted, rising slowly. He was glad to see the ice cracking around the edges. "You don't get to say what is or isn't enough here, Mr. Rock Star."

"Oh, please, let's try to keep this above juvenile insults," he said derisively.

"You had no right—"

"I'm the team leader—"

"Coleader, which means you get a vote. That doesn't mean you get to—"

"This isn't a class project with all the students getting a vote, Drucilla. It's a serious undertaking that's been years in the making and—"

"Since I'm the one who's devoted all those years to both the hypothesis and the proposed mathematical theory, I'm very well acquainted with the time involved here. What I'm not clear on is what gives you the right—"

"Right?" he yelled. "It's my name on this study that pulled in the funding. Which means it's my decision which funding we'll use, and how it'll be handled."

Alex gave her a "ha" smile. The I-won-the-interruption-game smile. The snotty, obnoxious, in-her-face triumphant smile.

Yeah, he was a dick. But it was damn hard to win an argument with Drucilla, so finally getting the last word meant he'd just scored major points.

And the fact that he was pathetically keeping score probably lost him a few of those points.

He winced, wondering how to apologize without giving up any ground.

"Look, Drucilla, you're a smart woman. A scientist who clearly understands the importance of making decisions based on well-documented, emotion-free, fact-based choices."

Tension pulled at his shoulder muscles as he watched her face for a reaction. When she didn't scrunch it up in anger, he relaxed a little. She unknotted her arms from in front of her and folded her hands at her waist.

Folded hands and unscrunched face. Good signs. He let his shoulders relax the rest of the way.

"Emotion free?" she asked. Then she stepped around the table, walked up close to him and laid her palm on his chest to stare up into his eyes. Alex's heart gave a huge sigh of happiness. "Emotion free is an interesting goal for the project, and for us, wouldn't you say?"

He smiled gratefully. She got it. She actually understood. Doing a manly happy dance was probably bad form at the moment, but he was definitely boogying mentally.

"Which is how you made this chickenshit, run-away-before-someone-realizes-you're-an-adult decision, right?" She gave his chest a stinging smack then stomped toward the door. "Because you're incapable of being mature enough to discuss the situation, let alone step up and consider what's good for anyone but yourself. To ask for one second what might be best for the project, for the team and, for God's sake, for the lab."

"Don't you mean for you?" he snarled, feeling blindsided. Chickenshit? He'd done this for her. And look what he got for hoping, for wishing. For risking his heart and thinking that maybe there could be something between them.

How many times did he have to be hit in the head to accept that while the sex might be awesome, it was only going to last as long as the next orgasm.

Or if her expression was anything to go by, the last.

14

SHE COULDN'T HAVE HEARD him right. Could she?

"You think I only care about myself?" Dru leaned against the table and blinked hard, trying to catch her breath after the pain his words caused.

"Isn't that what this is really about? You using a backer's deal to try to get me to stick around."

"What?"

"You must have realized Pownter would require us both to contract for the project. That she'd insist I stay around for the duration."

"You think I want to put my reputation, my career on the line so I can get you, your sexy body and your amazing lovemaking skills to stick around longer?"

Shock buzzed in her ears. Her eyes filled. From fury, she promised herself. And maybe just a little humiliation. Because, damn him, yes. That thought had crossed her mind. It wasn't the driving reason behind her choice, but it'd definitely been there.

And he'd just made it clear exactly how he felt about it.

She might cry, mourn and dive into a pint or six of Ben & Jerry's as soon as she got home. But she'd be damned if she'd let Alex know he'd just ripped her heart to pieces.

Alex, who had started her day with amazing sex, followed by fun and water games that'd nearly made her late for work.

Alex, who hadn't warned her that he'd spoken with the Trifecta director ahead of time and had known that the options she'd pitched during the team meeting were no longer available.

Alex, who had just left her tattered career in the dust kicked up by his swiftly retreating feet.

As hard as she tried, Dru couldn't find her usual icy composure to hide behind.

So instead she used the only protection she had left. She channeled all that hurt into blessed anger. She welcomed the fury churning in her gut. She knew it'd get her through this situation with her pride, and hopefully what tiny portion of her heart she had left, intact.

"Your ego is amazing," she breathed. "You know, I've studied your career. You've got this rock-star image, but you only stick around long enough to open for the real act. The ones who do the work and make an actual difference."

"Oh, please."

"No," she snapped before he could dismiss her. "You've got a brilliant mind, yes. But that doesn't mean jack. You never stay anyplace long enough to find out if you're actually any good."

"That's a lot of obsession with my career, isn't it," he accused in a mocking tone. "This is about you being jealous of my success and trying to tie me to this project."

"So let me get this straight," she clarified between clenched teeth. "You think I'd use this project to hold on to you? To trap you here, where you apparently hate to be, against your will?"

For one second, the shocked look of denial on his face was almost worth the misery spearing through her heart.

"I didn't mean it like that, Drucilla. I just don't want you thinking…"

"What, Alex? You don't want me thinking that you have faith in my abilities? That you actually want to work with me. Or even worse, that you want to see me, a woman you deemed good enough for sex but nothing else, stuck in a deal with a drunken cowboy instead of one of the largest institutes in the country."

"No," he snapped, finally losing that temper she'd wondered if he even had. "Quit twisting this around. I told you, this isn't about you. This is about me. I'm not the kind of guy who sticks around. You can't depend on me. I'm not future material."

Dru had to drop her gaze to blink the sudden tears from her eyes. Depend on him? When in her life had she ever been able to rely on a man?

And what kind of an idiot did it make her that he was right? She knew better. And still, she'd let herself fall in love.

"I was good enough to fall for on the beach," she said quietly, meeting his eyes again as soon as she'd regained control. "I was special enough to try to track down, to hope for some kind of longer relationship. But here now, in real life, you can't let yourself think about a future?"

Alex threw up his hand to wave that away as if he thought it was too stupid to acknowledge.

"Oh, please. Don't make this some big emotional scene. Back on the beach, you were a fantasy. Of course I wanted more."

Oh, wow, she'd thought she'd already hit rock bottom.

So this was what gut-punched felt like. Dru couldn't catch her breath. Stars did a queasy dance behind her eyes, making her want to hurl all over the boardroom table she'd so proudly presided over just a half hour ago.

"A fantasy?" she whispered. "That's all I was to you?"

"You were a fairy princess that I thought I could fall for," he muttered. Before her heart could even begin to hope, he continued, "Until reality hit."

"Reality," she said dully. And here she'd been so many kinds of thrilled that he still wanted her after he'd gotten to know the real her, the non-fantasy her. Where had she lost him? When he'd found out she was a scientist instead of a beach babe? When he'd met her mother? Or when she'd gotten all aggressive and done him against the wall of her apartment before he could take his coat off?

Dru shoved her hand through her hair, wondering how today had turned into her worst nightmare. What had happened to her confidence? Her anger? She needed one or the other, dammit, if she was going to get through this with any shred of dignity.

She looked at the boardroom table, the blue folder mocking her career hopes. And there it was. The tiny embers of anger. She thought of the Pownter deal. The huge career opportunities. A brand-new telescope and two years of funding.

And those embers flared.

"Well, I guess all we had was a fantasy," she said with an offhand shrug, pretending she wasn't miserable. "You got what you wanted and I got what I wanted."

"That's not—"

"You were looking for your fantasy," she interrupted. "And I was looking for mine."

He frowned.

"Yours?"

Dru had never been the revenge type. She'd never had a need to hurt a man before, either. But since she figured she probably wasn't strong enough to lift a chair over her head and get a satisfactory swing and do real damage, she used the only weapon she had.

"You were perfect fantasy material, Alex. A hot, sexy

beach stud." She watched his face turn a little paler and nodded. Oh, yeah. That hit home. "I had one goal for my vacation. To have a fling."

His brow furrowed and he shook his head.

"And you," she said with a nod as she pushed her luck and patted her palm against his bicep. "You were perfect fling material."

"You're not serious," he growled. "You're just saying that to piss me off."

"Why would you get pissed? You're not interested in a big emotional scene, remember?" she taunted.

"Stop it, Drucilla," he commanded, stalking over to sit, one-hipped, on the table. He gave her a cocky smile and shook his head. "You're trying to twist this around. You're obviously bent out of shape over my comment about you using me for work."

"You think I'm saying this because you accused me of sleeping with you to advance my career?"

"Hey!"

"Oh, what? It bothers you to be deemed only worthy of being a fantasy?" She looked him up and down as if he was a centerfold and she a horny housewife. "And yet, that's exactly what you were. A hot guy I saw on the beach who was all about sex. My very own boy toy."

He just glared.

"So thanks for the good time," she said when she reached the door and pulled it open. Then, unable to help herself, she stopped and looked back over her shoulder. "And hey, too bad you couldn't stick it out for the full three months."

Her chin trembled. It took all her strength to stiffen her jaw and continue, but she owed it to herself to get it all out.

"If you had, you might have found you liked it. I could have been the best damn thing to ever happen in your life, Alex. What we had, it might have been magic. I would have been someone you could count on. Someone who understood you. And even better, understood your work and your dreams and your brilliance. I could have been the one to give you everything you need. But you'll never know. You never gave it a chance." She sniffed, not even caring anymore that tears were streaming down her cheeks.

"You never gave us a chance. You say you're all about taking risks to achieve success. But that's a lie, Alex. You're so afraid of success—true, emotional success—that you run before the risk is even there."

She waited, one last desperate hope holding out for a response. But he just stared at her. That blank, shocked look of horror. As if she'd kicked him in the nuts.

Well, that worked. After all, he'd just kicked her in the heart.

With one last look, Dru shook her head and walked away.

Away from her career dreams.

Away from her newly found confidence.

Away from the man she loved.

ALEX STARED OUT at the crashing waves, searching for the peace of mind the ocean usually offered. The waters were grayer here, rough and wild. Beautiful in their own way, but not what he was used to.

And not, unfortunately, offering a semblance of peace.

All he could think of was that look of betrayal on Drucilla's face. The anger lurking in her eyes when she'd stormed out of the lab. God, he'd blown it. Better, though, to blow it now before she started thinking there was any chance of them having an actual relationship.

Which definitely made him a dick. He just wasn't sure how much of a dick he was. Or if size really mattered in this situation.

His cell phone buzzed, saving him from reaching any more depressing conclusions.

"Maddow."

"Baby."

Despite his gloom, Alex had to smile. "Hi, Mom."

"You feel jangly, baby. What's the matter?"

Feel, not sound. A lifetime of his mother's intuition meant Alex didn't blink at her knowing he was feeling like crap. The word *jangly,* though, did make him grin.

"Just some work problems."

"Are you working too hard, baby? You have to keep up the meditation routine. You know, yoga really isn't emasculating. My instructor is a very hunky and deliciously muscled man who mountain climbs, rides a very loud motorcycle and can go all night long."

Alex cringed. His mother's free-and-easy sexual dialogue with her only child? One of her less appealing qualities.

"I'll stick with the ocean," he said quickly.

"Which I can hear in the background, baby. So tell me what you're worrying about."

He shifted on the rock, feeling good for the first time in two days. His mom might be a little flaky, big on oversharing and unable to stay in one place for more than a month. But damned if she hadn't always been there for him.

"I'm thinking about heading to New York for a while," he said slowly, staring out at the pounding waves.

"New York? Too stuffy and fast, but you do better with the quicker pace than I do. So why are you thinking New York?"

"I was invited to join a physics group-lecture tour. They offered me keynote, but I can only stick with it for six weeks, then I'm heading to Maryland to consult for a month at Johns Hopkins."

"That's a lot of traveling, isn't it?"

"That's what we do," he said, grabbing a handful of small stones to lob into the ocean. "Make as much of an impact as possible as we travel the world, right?"

She made a sound of agreement, that mom sound that told him she was totally distracted but still paying attention.

"What about the cosmic string project?" she asked.

The rocks dug into his fingers as he fisted his hand in frustration. The waves were supposed to have washed this feeling away, weren't they?

He glared at the water and wondered if he should head down to Santa Cruz, maybe get some surfing in. He was much better as a participant than a spectator.

"Itchy feet," he sidestepped, using his mom's favorite excuse.

"Oh, baby." Disappointment dripped from her tone.

Alex pulled the phone away to give it a confused look, then grimaced and asked, "Huh?"

"You're not living up to your full potential, Albert Alexander."

Alex's automatic wince at his full name turned to confusion. "I repeat, huh?"

"You might be reaching your fullest scientific and career potential, but you're hiding from life."

Alex's spine stiffened. His mother's words stung, making him want to throw the phone this time instead of rocks.

"Isn't that why you're always on the go?" he asked. "To avoid things? To stay one step ahead of the mundane?"

"Mundane? Life should never be mundane, baby. If it is, you're doing something wrong."

"Then why do you always move around?" he asked, voicing the question that'd haunted him for most of his life, unable to stop the words this time.

"I love to see new things, new places. That was enough at first. Then, later, because I was thinking of you."

"Of me?"

"You're brilliant, baby. You always have been. At first, it was all I could give you. All I could show you. That there was a bigger world out there. That there is life outside the lab."

"I don't understand."

"Your father was just as obsessed with his job as your grandfather," she said, her voice sounding pained, as it always did when they talked about his father. "You know how intense your grandfather gets. He lives, breathes, eats for physics. His marriage failed, he has no friends and only sees you at science conferences."

"And Dad?"

"I'd love to think that if he'd survived, he'd have lived a full life. But he was already well on the road to following in your grandfather's footsteps. Work, work, work. All I could do was try to counteract that genetic obsession."

"And all your wanderings now?"

"Baby, I love to travel. I'm blessed that your father left me wealthy enough that I can do what I love without restriction. But that's for me. Not for you."

Alex unclenched his fist and stared at the indentations the rocks had left.

"Tell me this, do you like to travel, Albert Alexander?"

Alex winced again over the full name, but answered, "Not really."

"When you reach all those new places, do you sightsee? Do you collect mementos? Do you have photo albums?"

His sneer was an automatic rejection of girlie nostalgia, but he could still see where she was going with this.

"Albert Alexander?"

For the millionth time, Alex gave thanks that his mom called him by a juvenile nickname in all but the most serious discussions.

"No," he muttered.

"Baby, I wanted to give you a love for life. An openness to exploring possibilities. I never meant for you to become afraid of commitment."

"I'm not…"

"You don't even have an apartment," she said triumphantly, as if his lack of real estate was her ultimate proof.

"An apartment is hardly a sign of commitment, Mother. You never stay in yours."

"That's because it's not really there for me, baby. It's for you."

Alex squinted at the water, trying to figure that one out. Eventually he resorted to his fallback. "Huh?"

"You needed a place."

He couldn't even offer a *huh* to that.

"Well, face it, baby, we couldn't haul your awards around in the Chevy, could we?" When he didn't even laugh, she sighed, the sound huge over the phone.

"Look, I like moving around," Alex defended. "I thrive on the variety of challenges I encounter at the different labs and projects."

"Of course you do."

"And it helps that I don't make lasting connections. That kind of thing would just slow me down. Split my focus, you know?"

"And that's bad, right?"

"Well, yeah. How can I pay my dues to science if I'm giving it anything less than one hundred percent?"

"Your father used to say something similar."

Alex's arguments pretty well fizzled at that point. He stared at the water and tried to sort his thoughts.

"If I stick around, I'm bound to disappoint…someone."

"Life's full of disappointments, baby. The trick is to find someone who can help make those disappointments bearable.

Someone who makes you laugh, who gives you a reason to be thankful for each day and offers you the incentive to strive to be your best."

Bearable? Thankful? Be his best?

Instantly, Drucilla's face flashed in his mind. Her gorgeous eyes laughing up at him. The excitement she showed over his achievements and scientific genius. The sexual intensity she pushed him to, making him want to be bigger, stronger, better.

And it was just as simple as that.

"You bought the apartment for me?" he said, a little choked up.

"You need a touchstone. A home base and a sense of belonging. The apartment made you feel safe so you could have all those adventures."

Alex stared out at the pounding surf, finally feeling that inner peace the waves always brought him. Maybe it wasn't the ocean, he realized. Maybe it was that simple reminder of his actual touchstone.

"Thanks, Mom," he said quietly.

"You can always bring me these little problems. That's why I'm here. To take care of those things for you. Baby, you should know that by now."

He laughed.

"Now," she continued, "tell me about this girl you're all crazy in love with."

15

ALEX STRODE down the hall of Trifecta, filled with a sense of purpose. He paused in front of Drucilla's office door and wiped his hands on his jeans, then straightened his shoulders and reached for the doorknob.

Not that he had any doubts that Drucilla was going to be thrilled to see him…eventually. But the convincing part? That might be a little stressful.

But he was all about the challenge, he reminded himself as he knocked twice then twisted the knob.

"Drucilla," he greeted in such a fake jovial tone that it made him cringe internally.

Silence.

He scanned the office.

No gorgeous blonde behind the desk. No sexy scientist in the corner. No cried-on tissues overflowing the trash can. No shades pulled depressingly against the morning sunshine.

His shoulders slumped.

A part of him, so long in control, wanted to shrug and say, *"Hey, you tried. Now head off to the rest of your life."*

Then he thought about a future without Drucilla. If he walked away, that dismal image was a guarantee. The only chance he had to change it was to stick around long enough to convince her to give him a shot.

He threw himself into the chair and dropped his head against the wooden back with a heavy sigh. Crap, this all sucked so much. He'd blown it. He knew he had nobody else to blame, but that didn't stop him from wanting to smash something.

He'd spent the last two days trying to reach Drucilla, but she'd refused to answer the phone. He'd gone by her apartment, but if she'd been there hiding in the dark, she hadn't answered. He'd resisted—barely—stopping by her mother's.

But at this point, the only thing that'd kept him going through the night was the idea that he'd be able to fix things with Drucilla today.

So where the hell was she so he could get to the fixing?

Fingers tapping on the desk, he spent the first five minutes staring at the door.

He spent the next five pacing the office.

At the thirty-minute mark his nerves were shot, his hair a tousled mess and his stomach churning.

God, he had to get a grip. He slumped into Drucilla's chair, dug his elbows into the desk and dropped his head to his fists. Where the hell was she?

He stared at the folders neatly arranged under his elbows. His eyes narrowed. One, the thickest one, was labeled Pownter Contract.

Confused, he straightened and pulled it open. He'd barely started to read the first page when someone cleared her throat at the door.

"Drucilla," he said quickly, tossing the folder aside to jump up. He almost tripped over the chair as he hurried around the desk to greet her. So much for being smooth.

"I've been trying to reach you," he told her, not sure if he should be angry or relieved that she was finally here.

He stared, taking in the shock etched on that gorgeous face, and settled for thrilled.

"I got your messages," she said, looking anything but thrilled herself. Actually, she looked as if she wanted to turn tail and head right back out the door. After a couple seconds, though, she lifted her chin and stepped the rest of the way into the office, carefully shutting the door behind her.

"You got my messages?" he repeated. "But you didn't return them. Were you ever going to talk to me again?"

She wet her lips in that way that made him desperate to nibble on her. Then she shrugged and admitted, "I honestly hadn't planned to, no. I figured you were leaving and I was staying. What could we possibly have left to say to each other?"

He remembered the heart-wrenching words she'd thrown at him before walking out of the boardroom two days before. He'd been hoping he could breeze in here with a charming smile, a grand gesture, a pretty speech and that would fix everything. He'd figured he could sweep her off her feet again, without having to put himself too far out there.

But she deserved more than that.

They deserved more.

"Look, I screwed up," he declared. "I totally, selfishly screwed everything up. Us, the project, possibly our future. I'm here to do whatever is necessary to fix things between us."

"The reality hasn't changed, though, Alex." She said it as if she'd just confirmed a terminal prognosis. In a way, hadn't she? Because if her expression was any indication, she considered their relationship dead and buried.

"I can fix the reality," he insisted.

"You can't change me, Alex."

"Huh?" What the hell was she talking about? And he was supposed to be such a brilliant guy?

"You said you were totally into me until reality hit. Until you got to know the real me," she said. The pain those words had caused was clear in her voice, the devastation making her lower lip tremble.

"You think that's the reality I was talking about? That that's what I meant?" he asked slowly. God, he was such a dick. He'd been so busy trying to run before he got hurt, he hadn't seen the pain he was causing Drucilla.

He could see it now, though. Her beautiful indigo eyes were filled with pain. He couldn't stop his move toward her any more than he could stop his next breath.

"I didn't mean you," he explained, risking her anger but not able to help himself from taking her hands and lifting them to his lips. "You, Drucilla, are perfect. You're sweet and sexy. Smart and savvy. You're clever, loving and loyal. The reality of you is more than my heart can hold."

"But... I don't understand." She looked as if he'd just smacked her upside the head with a telescope. Wide-eyed, shocked and still a little hurt.

"I meant my reality, Drucilla," he said quickly, needing to get that look off her face.

She sniffed, pressing her lips tight. He could see her trying to find the icy cloak she used to hide behind. But with her hands trembling in his, she couldn't seem to.

"I don't understand," she repeated. She offered him a shaky smile then said in a joking tone, "Are we talking about perception or multidimensional realities here?"

"I'm the problem. You were right," he explained. Even though he knew he had to get the words out, saying them was harder than taking a surfboard to the head. "This is my issue. I thought I had to move from place to place. That I couldn't commit to anything. My dad was a physicist. My grandfather's a physicist. Both of them were barely able to commit long enough to sire children, let alone anything else."

He forced himself to push past a lifelong loyalty and, he finally admitted, just as many years of lying to himself. "My parents had a lousy marriage. They were in the process of divorcing when my dad died in a plane crash. He was never home anyway, so I barely noticed the difference."

She gave him a long, sympathetic look as she gently slid her hands over his cheeks. Pressing a soft kiss to his lips, she leaned back and told him, "I understand. I really do. I spent most of my life thinking I was just like my father—doomed to fail."

He smoothed his hand through her hair and pressed his own kiss to her forehead, wondering how two seemingly intelligent people could be so emotionally stupid.

"I take it you've realized how mistaken that thinking is," he said with a stern look.

Her smile was hesitant, but it still felt like sunshine, warming him all the way through to his heart.

"I did," she admitted. "Even better, I realized that the only failures I'm accountable for are my own, and the only person who can drive my success is me."

He nodded, tucking her hair behind her ear so he could better see the clean lines of her beautiful face.

"I wasn't trying to derail your success, or undermine your authority, Drucilla. Please keep that in mind…" He hesitated, wanting to let it go. But he'd learned his lesson before. He had to tell her right away. "But I tried to contact Charlene Pownter yesterday. I was going to offer to accept the original contract. Complete with the two-year agreement."

"What?" She stared up at him as if he really was the rock star she always referred to him as. Awed, shocked and just a little turned on. He liked that look.

He was torn between kissing her while she stared up a him like that and hurrying on with the details. As much a

wanted her, he wanted to get on with their future together
en more.

"I tried to get the deal back for you. I figured if I agreed to
ms, maybe offered to do a few additional lectures or assist
any of their other projects, they might reconsider."

"Alex—"

"No, don't thank me or anything," he interrupted. "I
uldn't reach Charlene so nothing's set yet. But I will, I
omise." And he would. He'd do anything for her. "Or I'll
er whatever you prefer. I just want this to work out, for us
work together. To be together."

, GOD. It was like having a dream come true right here in
office. The only thing that kept her from pinching herself
see if she was really asleep was the fact that they were
th fully clothed. Generally, all her dreams of Alex had at
.st one of them mostly naked.

Dru scrunched her nose, nibbling at her lower lip as she
ed to figure out how to answer him without damaging his
. Or worse, driving another wedge between them.

"Alex, I appreciate that. I really do." She tore her gaze from
face, with those dark sexy eyes watching her so intently,
l waved her hand toward her desk. "But, well, I've already
eed to a different contract."

He frowned, looking at the Pownter-contract folder she'd
stured to. She winced, waiting.

"I'm not sure I understand," he said slowly.

She had to move. But she couldn't pace in a room that felt
if it'd shrunk in half, so she had to settle for twisting her
gers together. There had to be a good way to explain and
l keep what was looking like a dream come true.

"I really wanted the Pownter deal," she told him. "It was,
me at least, a once-in-a-lifetime shot. I wasn't willing to
let it go. Especially not when you…"

"When I bailed on the entire project?"

She nodded. "Right. Well, I took a chance and met wit Charlene. Actually with her full board. I talked to them convinced them to accept Trifecta under a slightly differer contract than they'd originally offered."

His proud smile warmed her through and through.

"You faced that entire board and pitched a new deal? That excellent. I'll bet you were incredible. They must have bee eating out of your hand."

Her shoulders straightened just a little and she gave him a excited smile. "I wouldn't say that, but they were definitel receptive. There are a few changes to the deal, though. I don know if they're changes you'll be okay with."

He lifted her hand to his lips and pressed a kiss, heate and damp, against the palm of her hand. She could feel th tingles all the way to her toes.

"I'll do anything, Drucilla. For you. For us. And—" h grinned a little over the finger he was nibbling on "—to te you the truth, I'd rather commit to the Pownter Institute tha Blackstone."

Dru gave him a feeble smile and searched deeper for th right words. It was hard, though, with him playing sexy suc ing games with her fingers.

"Alex, I love that you were willing to try to change Tr fecta's deal for me. I love even more that you'd be willing take on a two-year contract to prove that you're serious abou sticking around. But—"

"No," he interrupted. "No buts."

"But," she insisted, "this new contract was negotiated wit the idea that you were off the team. I was able to convinc Charlene that I was good enough, strong enough, to lead th project. She's willing to take a risk on me. The same deal a she originally offered Trifecta, but with me, just me—" sh took a deep breath before continuing "—in charge."

He went still. Her fingers tensed.

"I still want you on the team, if you're willing to work with me," she said quickly. "Your input and participation would be invaluable. Even if you weren't, you know, the leader of record."

"I'd be working under you?" he clarified.

She nodded, braced for his reaction.

Then he laughed. A slow chuckle at first, then a deep guffaw. She stared, baffled. How was that funny?

"Well, I do like it when you're on top," he told her with a wicked look in his dark eyes.

Her sigh came out as a giggle as she smiled up at him.

"I love how enthusiastic you are about the potential work," she teased.

He stopped grinning and gave her a long, serious look, as if he was trying to find the right way to tell her something. She held her breath, staring up at him.

"You're using the word *love* an awful lot today," he commented with an inscrutable look.

"Not to scare you," she blurted. Regretfully, she pulled her fingers from his to grip his arms in case he decided to storm out. "I wasn't trying to…"

"I know," he said, wrapping his now-free hands around her waist and pulling her tighter against his body. She sighed in pleasure at the wonderful feeling of him pressed against her again. "Actually, I like hearing it. It's not a word I'm overly familiar with, though."

What was he getting at? Dru wished desperately that she'd skipped breakfast, since the wild dance of nerves going on in her belly was making her a little queasy.

"It's not an emotion I'm used to, either," he admitted, confirming the direction he was heading and scaring the hell out of her. Dru was torn between running from her deepest desire and pushing him to hurry along the confession.

Push, she decided, going for broke. She wanted the confession.

With that in mind, she leaned in closer to his body and, releasing his arms, curved her palms over his cheeks. She gave him her sexiest—albeit a little shaky and nauseous—smile and stood on her tiptoes to kiss him.

Before she could reach his lips, though, he put his hands on her shoulders to halt the forward momentum.

"So you nailed the deal on your own?" he clarified, staring at her.

Dru nodded. Weren't they supposed to be tossing around that scary *L* word?

Nervous again, she folded her lips together and waited to see if his *L* word was strong enough, real enough, for *her* reality.

"And you don't need me to advance your career?"

She shook her head so quickly, her hair whipped at both their faces.

"But I'm welcome to hang around, continue to colead the team and participate in the project?"

Dru's stomach sank, tears welling in her eyes even though she wasn't sure why. She gave a tiny nod and held her breath.

Alex heaved a deep sigh and closed his eyes, letting his head fall back for a moment.

"This actually creates a problem," he said after a few seconds.

"What kind of…? How…? What do you mean a problem?" she finally blurted out.

"I figured I'd swoop in here and save your career," he told her. "That you'd be so grateful, you'd overlook my asinine behavior and welcome me back with open arms."

She gave a relieved laugh, only tinged a bit with hysteria.

"I figured the project, and the mandatory two-year commitment, would serve as some sort of testament. But instead, you've eliminated my easy, waltz-in-and-be-a-hero-while-taking-minimal-responsibility commitment."

Dru opened her mouth, but didn't know what to say. She closed it, then opened it again and offered, "I'm sorry?"

"You should be." He pulled her into his arms so fast, she squeaked. Laughter and joy twined together, filling her with happiness. "Now you're going to have to pay, you know."

"How?" she asked as she wreathed her arms around his neck and snuggled closer with a happy sigh.

"By loving me," he said against her hair. "I'm talking long-term here, Drucilla. No fantasy stuff. Just you, me and reality."

She tilted her head back to smile up at him.

"I do," she said. "I love you today, I'll love you tomorrow and all the tomorrows after."

Finally, his mouth met hers, their kiss a sweet affirmation to their professed feelings. The gentle, almost reverent glide of lips made Dru tremble inside.

She pulled away just a little and gave him a naughty look.

"But the deal is, we keep the fantasies. After all, I'm imagining you right now, naked on the desk."

"You're the boss," he agreed with that sexy, beach god smile she'd fallen so hard for. Then he gave her a wink and leaned down for a kiss.

"No," she said quietly.

Alex blinked, but he didn't say anything.

"We're partners," she told him, a little giddy at the idea of being so wonderfully in love. "That means we're both the boss."

Epilogue

EXHILARATION SURGED through Drucilla's body. Muscles tight, she filled her lungs with the warm evening air then gave a deep sigh of satisfaction.

There was nothing like surfing at sunset. The colors of the sky, the feel of the cooling air as it whipped around her body while she flew over the water. Incredible. Simply incredible. Much like her life.

"Are you ready?" Alex asked from his own board a few feet from hers. "You sure you want to take this on? These waves are bigger than you're used to."

Dru's joyful laughter bounced off the water and she shook her head, droplets spraying around her like a halo. "Oh, yeah, I can handle it."

She could handle anything.

The wave built, its roar filling her ears. The diamond of her wedding ring glinted in the sun as she gripped the sides of the board. Her body tensed, not in dread but in wild anticipation. This was it. Time to give herself over to the pleasure of riding the waves. Second only to her favorite ride—Alex.

A ride all her own.

* * * * *

COMING NEXT MONTH

Available September 28, 2010

REQUEST YOUR FREE BOOKS!

2 FREE NOVELS PLUS 2 FREE GIFTS!

HARLEQUIN®

Blaze

Red-hot reads!

YES! Please send me 2 FREE Harlequin® Blaze™ novels and my 2 FREE gifts (gifts are worth about $10). After receiving them, if I don't wish to receive any more books, I can return the shipping statement marked "cancel." If I don't cancel, I will receive 6 brand-new novels every month and be billed just $4.24 per book in the U.S. or $4.71 per book in Canada. That's a saving of at least 15% off the cover price. It's quite a bargain. Shipping and handling is just 50¢ per book.* I understand that accepting the 2 free books and gifts places me under no obligation to buy anything. I can always return a shipment and cancel at any time. Even if I never buy another book, the two free books and gifts are mine to keep forever.

151/351 HDN E5LS

Name _____ (PLEASE PRINT) _____

Address _____ Apt. #

City _____ State/Prov. _____ Zip/Postal Code

Signature (if under 18, a parent or guardian must sign)

Mail to the **Harlequin Reader Service:**
IN U.S.A.: P.O. Box 1867, Buffalo, NY 14240-1867
IN CANADA: P.O. Box 609, Fort Erie, Ontario L2A 5X3

Not valid for current subscribers to Harlequin Blaze books.

Want to try two free books from another line?
Call 1-800-873-8635 or visit www.morefreebooks.com.

* Terms and prices subject to change without notice. Prices do not include applicable taxes. N.Y. residents add applicable sales tax. Canadian residents will be charged applicable provincial taxes and GST. Offer not valid in Quebec. This offer is limited to one order per household. All orders subject to approval. Credit or debit balances in a customer's account(s) may be offset by any other outstanding balance owed by or to the customer. Please allow 4 to 6 weeks for delivery. Offer available while quantities last.

Your Privacy: Harlequin Books is committed to protecting your privacy. Our Privacy Policy is available online at www.eHarlequin.com or upon request from the Reader Service. From time to time we make our lists of customers available to reputable third parties who may have a product or service of interest to you. If you would prefer we not share your name and address, please check here. ☐

Help us get it right—We strive for accurate, respectful and relevant communications. To clarify or modify your communication preferences, visit us at www.ReaderService.com/consumerschoice.

HB10R

HARLEQUIN®

A *Romance*

FOR EVERY MOOD™

Spotlight on

Inspirational

Wholesome romances
that touch the heart and soul.

See the next page
to enjoy a sneak peek from
the Love Inspired® inspirational series.

*See below for a sneak peek at
our inspirational line, Love Inspired®.
Introducing HIS HOLIDAY BRIDE
by bestselling author Jillian Hart*

Autumn Granger gave her horse rein to slide toward the town's new sheriff.

"Hey, there." The man in a brand-new Stetson, black T-shirt, jeans and riding boots held up a hand in greeting. He stepped away from his four-wheel drive with "Sheriff" in black on the doors and waded through the grasses. "I'm new around here."

"I'm Autumn Granger."

"Nice to meet you, Miss Granger. I'm Ford Sherman, from Chicago." He knuckled back his hat, revealing the most handsome face she'd ever seen. Big blue eyes contrasted with his sun-tanned complexion.

"I'm guessing you haven't seen much open land. Out here, you've got to keep an eye on cows or they're going to tear your vehicle apart."

"What?" He whipped around. Sure enough, mammoth black-and-white creatures had started to gnaw on his four-wheel drive. They clustered like a mob, mouths and tongues and teeth bent on destruction. One cow tried to pry the wiper off the windshield, another chewed on the side mirror. Several leaned through the open window, licking the seats.

"Move along, little dogie." He didn't know the first thing about cattle.

The entire herd swiveled their heads to study him curiously. Not a single hoof shifted. The animals soon returned to chewing, licking, digging through his possessions.

Autumn laughed, a warm and wonderful sound. "Thanks,

I needed that." She then pulled a bag from behind her saddle and waved it at the cows. "Look what I have, guys. Cookies."

Cows swung in her direction, and dozens of liquid brown eyes brightened with cookie hopes. As she circled the car, the cattle bounded after her. The earth shook with the force of their powerful hooves.

"Next time, you're on your own, city boy." She tipped her hat. The cowgirl stayed on his mind, the sweetest thing he had ever seen.

Will Ford be able to stick it out in the country
to find out more about Autumn?
Find out in HIS HOLIDAY BRIDE
by bestselling author Jillian Hart,
available in October 2010
only from Love Inspired®.

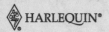